need

Also by Robert Thomson

Secret Things

need

stories

Robert Thomson

The Riverbank Press

Cover and text design: John Terauds

THE CANADA COUNCIL | LE CONSEIL DES ARTS
FOR THE ARTS | DU CANADA
SINCE 1957 | DEPUIS 1957

We acknowledge the support of the
Canada Council for the Arts for our
publishing program.

Canadian Cataloguing in Publication Data

Thomson, Robert (Robert Walter), 1964-
    Need : stories

ISBN 1-896332-10-2

I. Title.

PS8589.H5387N43 1999   C813' .54   C99-931413-0
PR9199.3.T46N43 1999

Lyrics quoted in "For the Love of Ella"
from "Who's Sorry Now?" written by Snyder/Kalmar/Ruby

First published by
The Riverbank Press
P.O. Box 456, 31 Adelaide St. East
Toronto, Ontario, Canada M5C 2J5

Printed and bound in Canada by Métrolitho

To Michael and James, without whom I would be lost.

acknowledgements

James Johnstone, Mark Rosenbauer,
Brian Davis, Stephen Nunn, Mark Du Pont,
Michael Thomas Ford, Dean Odorico, Steven Clegg,
Kenneth Blochowski, Brian Lam, John Terauds,
Attila Berki: Thanks for your friendship, support,
encouragment, and valuable lessons.

Some of the material in this book has been previously published, although in a slightly altered form: "Bad Emotional Risk" was published in *Quickies 2* (Arsenal Pulp Press); "Everything" was published in *Best Gay Erotica 1998* (Cleis Press); and "Waiting" was performed as a monologue in "An Evening of Music and Comedy 4" and "Waiting."

contents

an introduction of sorts

We stand alone, together, clinging to each other, caught in the headlights of life, convinced that no matter which way we turn, reality will run us over.

Instead of jumping off tall buildings, we jump off people; lovers, friends, family, anything to up the volume, sharpen the pain, improve the drama. We jump to and from conclusions, leaping to temporary deaths, drowning in pools of adrenaline.

We are not separate, hidden from you. We move about you, in transit, in transition. We want and wait and wish and wonder if anyone knows if and why we're alive.

The world spins around us while we spin around in our worlds.

maria von frank n. trap furter

Three years ago, late on Christmas Eve, my telephone rang. It was Norman. He had just come out to his family — bad timing, I thought. They had rejected him and then ejected him from their house before he could even collect his presents. Since then we have reintroduced ourselves to each other and learned what is considered acceptable conversation and what is off limits. I was chaperone to Norman's first foray into gay life, a preppy bar filled with subtly leering eyes. I was there when Norman met his first boyfriend. I was there after Norman told him goodbye. I introduced Norman to his second boyfriend, Gabriel, the one he lived with until three months ago. I was there when Gabriel dumped him. During the past three years I've done more than one hundred shows at various clubs and small theatres in Toronto. Norman hasn't seen a single one.

When Norman is alone, he spends most of his time cleaning and making lists: lists of things he owns; things he would like to own; lists of places he's been and would like to visit; people he knows and would like to meet.

Norman's apartment is immaculate. He has a two-month supply of socks and underwear. This way, he figures he won't have to spend as much time doing laundry. The clothes in his closet are arranged by colour; shirts on the top four shelves – lighter shades on top, darker on the bottom; pants, socks and underwear on the bottom four shelves. And in the back of the closet sits a small safe. In a rare moment of self-revelation, Norman showed me his stash. Inside this safe are pornographic magazines, the expensive kind, filled with glossy pictures of man-boys bending over, pouting, touching themselves.

I barely own a week's supply of socks and can often be found doing laundry. I store my socks and underwear on any shelf in my closet, or on the floor, where they're easier to find. I keep a journal, but usually only when something of extreme importance happens: a new dress; a new man who is interested in me *after* he finds out I put on makeup and women's clothes; when I travel; re-enter therapy. Through the years I have accumulated five volumes of journals filled with spontaneous thoughts, poems, the names of all the men I've had sex with and the dates when I've quit smoking. (Sometimes the two are connected.) I own two magazines containing pictures of naked men. They used to be under my bed, but I'm not quite sure where they are now.

I spend a great deal of time worrying that things I say might offend people and that they're too polite to let me know. And although I used to consider myself to be unemotive, over the last few years I've discovered that the opposite is true – at least when I'm in drag.

When it comes to relationships, I have a sordid past. I haven't had one that's lasted longer than two months. That's usually how long it takes for the reality of my "other persona" to sink in and for the man to make a quick get-away. I am twenty-nine, have a nasty drag habit, and live in a second-floor walk-up in Toronto. I'm used to being ignored. *Tant pis*, as they say in French. Tough luck. Or as I prefer to say, Aunt Piss.

"I'm not looking anymore," I'll tell a friend at a bar as my head spins back and forth, my eyes scanning the room. Yes, I often contradict myself. I am flawed.

Norman, however, is perfect. He spends a lot of time and effort going through his wardrobe and selecting what to wear before going out at night. Cute young things seem to gravitate toward him. And since he and Gabriel broke up, Norman has been going out a lot.

Norman goes to homes, apartments and warehouses. He goes to underwear parties where you check much more than your coat at the door. He is always surrounded by the same attractive, shirtless men, the same men he once confessed frightened him, made him think that fags were decadent and self-indulgent. Norman has a need to be accepted, to be admired. I know that Norman is very lonely deep down. And Norman knows I know. That knowledge has all but destroyed a friendship that has undergone as many changes as the two men in it.

Norman and I met during our last year at high school, on the yearbook committee, and became school chums for a while. One day I suggested we catch a screening of *The Sound Of Music* at one of the repertory cinemas. Neither one of us had seen it in its entirety on a large screen since our childhood.

Norman picked me up in his parents' car.

I pulled a tape out of my pocket and slid it into the deck, sending "I Want Candy" by Bow Wow Wow out the speakers. Norman reached over and turned the volume down, giving me a disapproving frown.

"Do you think they'll cut any scenes like they do on TV?" he asked.

"Of course not! They only do that so they can stick in enough commercials."

"Oh, good," Norman sighed. "I wouldn't want to miss the waltz scene."

"I know! Don't you just love it when Maria blushes? It's such a great scene! But my favourite part is the puppet show."

"No way, Donnie! 'Do-Re-Mi' is the best."

"No, wait, wait! What about the opening?"

"Yeah! How could we forget the opening?"

And so we bantered until we had settled into our seats.

"They'd never get away with seats like this where I work," Norman said.

"Yeah, but your theatre charges more than twice the admission."

The Kingsway was a rep cinema in the west end. Admission was cheap, they served real butter on the popcorn, and refreshments rarely cost more than the admission price.

Within a few minutes, the house lights dimmed and a pair of blood-red lips filled the screen. It was a trailer for

The Rocky Horror Picture Show.

Tim Curry, larger than life, threw off his black cape to reveal high glittery heels, fishnet stockings, garters and corset and sang "I'm just a sweet transvestite."

"It's a freak show," Norman mumbled as he shifted in his seat.

"I know!" I said enthusiastically. "I want to see it."

"Just don't ask me to go with you."

From then on, I spent each and every Friday and Saturday night seeing *Rocky Horror* at the more hip downtown rep cinema, the Roxy. Norman joined the youth group at our high school.

I'll never forget my excitement during *The Sound of Music*'s opening sequence. As the music swelled, our anticipation grew, finally rewarded by Julie Andrews walking toward us on the mountaintop. Julie spun around, arms out, and burst gloriously into "The hills are alive ..."

Somewhere between Tim Curry in drag and Julie Andrews in a nun's habit, there was an irrevocable click.

My obsession with *The Rocky Horror Picture Show* grew with each viewing. My parents responded with grim displeasure to the numerous posters of Dr. Frank N. Furter in full drag, those deep-red lascivious lips, and the film's title in dripping-blood letters that I put up in my bedroom. It probably didn't help that the other movie posters included *Halloween*, *Phantasm*, and *Fame*. What was I turning into, an undead singing transvestite serial killer who wanted to open on Broadway? Who was to blame for my descent into decadence, madness and cross-dressing in lingerie? Tim Curry? Julie Andrews? My parents?

Twentieth-Century Fox?

Unlike good-student Norman, who got the highest GPA in our class, I wouldn't be attending university in the fall, and accepted a full-time job as a short-order cook at a local greasy spoon, at least for the summer. It was here that I fell in love for the first time, with a handsome black boy my age named Daniel.

I made a new circle of friends, got up the courage to tell Daniel how I felt about him, and stumbled out of the closet. He was there to catch me, but only stayed until I was standing on my feet again. He could accept the fact that I loved him, but not that I wanted to have sex with him. My obsession grew. By September, all my friends at the restaurant – Daniel included – had returned to school, Norman had moved to Montreal to attend Concordia University, and I continued making omelettes and burgers during the day, Monday through Friday, waiting for life to throw me a curve ball and give me the opportunity to strike wildly at it.

"Our next contestant is well known to you all, I'm sure. Currently in town filming *Hell Night Part Two: The Devil Made Me Do It*, please welcome to our stage the star of *Roller Booger*, Linda Blur!"

The Sunday Night Freak Show at Chaps was an evening of hysterical, inventive, and sometimes pathetic drag. I chose the show's first anniversary for my début. The upstairs bar was packed. I had never seen so many people at a drag show in my life. I was throwing back tequila when I heard the announcement.

The crowd didn't know how to respond when I came on wearing a nun's habit, carrying a guitar in one hand and a can of pea soup in the other. I sat myself on a stool in the centre of the stage just as the music started. It was the opening of "Do-Re-Mi." I pretended to pluck at the guitar, lipsynching Julie Andrews perfectly. "Let's start at the very beginning ..." After about a minute, just after Julie says, "Oh let's see if I can make it easier," the music stopped, and Linda Blair's demonic voice from *The Exorcist* shouts out, "Your mother sucks cocks in hell!" I started to shake and quake, and "Tubular Bells" started playing. I'd dubbed parts of the soundtrack of *The Exorcist* over the eerie music. So while I was on stage tugging at my costume, Linda Blair was screaming, "Mother, make it stop! Fuck me!" Then I pulled out the crucifix I had hidden in my costume and started kissing it and licking it and rubbing it against my chest and between my legs. Some people in the audience were booing. Others were laughing hysterically and clapping. There was so much noise I got kind of lost and wound up throwing myself to the floor, writhing about with the crucifix between my legs, with Linda Blair's distorted voice grunting, "Your mother sucks cocks in hell" repeatedly as I slithered on the stage floor. The music faded out. I stood up, brushed myself off and, with my guitar in hand, left the stage with a polite bow. The can of pea soup remained on the stool.

I came in second. And I had made an impression. Months later, I hosted my own show ("Anesta Whorenets'

Unstoppable Whore Tour") at Chaps. I came onstage dressed as Frank N. Furter with a bottle of Kwelada in one hand and a microphone in the other, and sang to a Karaoke tape of "My Favorite Things."

> ...*When the crabs bite*
> *When the pee stings*
> *When my luck is bad*
> *I simply remember my favorite flings*
> *And then I don't feel so sad...*

I pick up the phone on it's third ring, while scanning the room for cigarettes.

"Hello?"

"I'm exhausted. I just got home from this party. It was great. I met this really cute guy named Lou."

"A cute guy named Lou? Isn't that a contradiction in terms?"

"He's in the bathroom throwing up."

"How romantic!"

"We didn't have sex, though."

"Of course not. Why spoil the show?"

"Well, we couldn't, really. We were too drunk. I still am."

"Norman —"

"I know. We did sleep together, though. Do you know that this is only the third time I've been in bed with someone since Gabriel?"

"What about the guys you cheated with? Don't they

count?"

"No. I was still with Gabriel when I slept with them. Besides, I'm not talking about sex, I'm talking about just sleeping with the guy."

"Oh," I say, thinking how my apartment is a mess.

"Anyway, we only got like two hours of sleep and then Perry called and invited me to the opera tonight. That's why I'm calling. I don't think I'm going to be able to make dinner."

"Norman! I was just about to get dressed. We're supposed to meet in forty-five minutes."

"I know. Sorry. But it's the only chance I'll get to see *Tosca*. The run is sold out. I just hope Perry and his friends won't be able to smell the alcohol on me."

I don't respond.

"It's actually good that we didn't have sex, I think. I don't really want to get involved with anybody right now. Maybe its too soon after Gabriel ..."

I'm confused. Taking someone home, sleeping with them – sleeping – letting them vomit in your bathroom ... That isn't being involved?

"You've ruined my Saturday night. Again."

"If you're upset then I suppose I could cancel the opera."

"No, why bother? You've made your priorities quite clear."

"Are you angry?"

"Of course I'm angry! I'm so fucking angry I could scream!"

"You are screaming."

"Well, then I'm angry, aren't I?"

"Donnie, we can have dinner any night. The opera is a special event."

"Do you know how many times you've done this to me?"

"No."

"Countless times, Norman. You don't even notice, do you? It's probably never even occurred to you."

"I guess ... I'm sorry."

"Norman, let me tell you something else. Remember when you and Gabriel were together and you used to have those parties and you never invited me because they were for couples only, but you always told me about them?"

"Yeah?"

"And how if I ever got invited to your place I was the only guest?"

"Yeah."

"Why did you do that? I mean, is it about me? Because of the drag thing?"

"Um, I don't know. I don't think so."

"Do you know how shitty it made me feel?"

"Uh, no. I guess we didn't. Do you want me to apologize?"

"Don't strain yourself." I let the receiver fall into the cradle.

I am at the plastic surgeon's office. Dr. Lichtman and I are meeting for the first time. I've brought pictures of what I want to have done. Two years of saving money have finally brought me here. I open the envelope and remove a number of pictures in various sizes. First the lips. I've freeze-framed my *Rocky Horror* laserdisc and photographed the lips from the opening credits. I want those lips. Dr. Lichtman glances at the photos, then back at me. He raises an eyebrow and tilts his head.

"You want these lips?"

"Those lips, yeah. Uh-huh."

He drops the pictures on the desk. "What else?"

I hand him five more pictures, some broad shots, some extreme closeups.

"Oh, Julie Andrews," he says.

"Yes. I want her nose."

"Really?" He looks at my face again and then back at Julie's. "Well, this is certainly a challenge."

"Is it possible?"

"Yes, but it may take some time."

"How long"

"It depends on how long you take to heal. Are you sure you want to do this?"

"Sure I'm sure."

Then he starts showing me pictures of the procedures, a slice-and-dice collage designed to scare away flakes and weirdos. It works. I decide to abandon that project and put a down payment on a townhouse instead. Instead of being fabulous, I will become a homeowner, which is probably a better thing in the long run.

Other things needed to change, too. When I realized how boring some of the city's drag queens were at performing, I decided to highlight my ability to sing, not just lipsynch like some fourteen-year-old wannabe in the bathroom mirror. It was time for a new look, name, and attitude. So I got all done up one night at home, looked into the mirror, and started removing, bit by bit, the things that were clownish, while blaring Alanis Morissette's *Supposed Former Infatuation Junkie* on the stereo.

An hour later I had nothing but cold cream on my face.

"It's my pleasure to introduce to you tonight, in her first public drag performance in over five years, Anesta Whorenets, singing live!"

As I stepped up to the stage (you call two milk cartons a stage?) the emcee handed me the microphone and whispered a word of encouragement.

My costume was average: a huge, swirling black sequined cape, and an enormous headdress. I placed the microphone down beside my feet, and stood up again to face the crowd. I lifted off the headdress and let it fall to the floor. The audience made approving noises. Then I opened the cape, and pulled it off, leaving a pair of tight leather pants, a plain black T-shirt, black parade boots (used, of course, and unlaced), and a waist-length mane of straight black hair.

The audience started clapping and hooting. Piano keys struck out the eight opening notes of Morissette's "Are You Still Mad." The audience roared.

Are you still mad I kicked you in the crotch?
Are you still mad I gave you STDs?
Are you still mad I compared you to all
     the guys who couldn't make me come?
Are you still mad I used our condoms with everybody?

Are you still mad I had no emotional response?
Are you still mad I tried to steal your VCR and your DVD?
Are you still mad I didn't like your best intentions?
Of course you are, of course you are, of course you are.

Are you still mad that I flirted with your best friend?
Are you still mad I had a tendency to be a mother fucker?
Are you still mad I had both feet in my mouth?
Are you still mad that we kept fucking even after
     I infected you?
Of course you are, of course you are, of course you are.

Are you still mad I was in drag most of the time?
Are you still mad that I seemed to focus only on your many faults?
Are you still mad that I stole your towels?
Are you still mad that I gave them to my new boyfriend?
Of course you are, of course you are, of course you are.

I retired Anesta Whorenets after four shows. Even though it was 1999, the closing days of what I call the decade of anger, this wasn't an attractive emotion for a queen to display, and drunk homosexuals don't want to process crafty lyrics. I decided to take some time off from the stage.

◊   ◊   ◊

I dragged myself away from my sabbatical for a special resurrection of my Maria von Frank N. Trap Furter routine at a celebrity lookalike contest. The number I did was "The Sound of Music."

As the music began its crescendo, I spun around, the carpetbag and guitar case gripped firmly in my out-stretched arms. Two steps back from centre stage I dropped my props, and, just as Julie Andrew's voice was about to chime out "The hills are alive," I pulled the Velcroed nun's habit off in one quick movement to reveal sparkled platform shoes, fishnets, black lace underwear, a purple sequined corset, and a string of large pearls around my neck. The heavy guitar intro to "Sweet Transvestite" cut in and I was on my way. The audience screamed and applauded.

Ever since my mother took me to see *The Sound of Music* as a child, I've wanted to be Julie Andrews. Tim Curry was the most masculine, engaging man I'd ever seen. I envied Frank N. Furter's ferocity and vulnerability. The Holly-wood dream machine created a monster in me. I am free-dom and oppression, God and Satan, Bibles and vibrators. I am Maria Von Frank N. Trapp Furter, society's best and worst all at once.

I checked my answering machine when I got home from the club. The first two calls were hang-ups. The third message was from Norman.

"I saw your show tonight, Donnie. You're pathetic. Really pathetic! I would think that you'd have better judgment than to appear in public like that. For years I've tried to avoid looking at this part of you, and now I know why. You're a freak. And I suspected it all along. Since high school. And I talked to Gabriel a little while ago and he said that you were the reason he broke up our relationship. Apparently you told him I was screwing around on him every chance I could get. So you're a freak, and you betrayed me. I don't want to be your friend anymore. So don't call me, and if I see you in public, just ignore me, okay? You're the reason people hate fags and I don't blame them! Goodbye."

There was a beep. The tape in the machine stopped whirring and I stood frozen in my kitchen, wondering if I was supposed to feel bad or guilty or ashamed. Because I didn't.

I know why Norman's lover left him — and it wasn't because I told him Norman was cheating on him. Gabriel already knew. He suspected, asked me, and I confirmed it. Gabriel's reason for leaving was that Norman wasn't the man he thought he was. And Gabriel realized that an ideal man does not exist. Gabriel dates now, occasionally, and dreams of understanding his tastes. He is single because he chooses to be. I am single because of the life I have chosen for myself. And I am rarely lonely. Norman is single because he is all surface and façade. Deep inside, he believes that he is all that is base and vile about Frank N. Furter and that he has to act like Maria Von Trapp in order to atone for it.

Although I am not whole, I at least have two halves. Norman, I think, will be forever fragmented, always trying to charm people who want and need him to be normal. Through their eyes, he can realize his dreams. But in the mirror, he does not know who or what he sees. And I am not Norman's mirror, although I am probably one of the few people who has an accurate picture of him. I don't know what would have happened to me had I tried to be respectable, or accepted, or loved. Chances are I would have wound up exactly where I am. And I'm more than successful, more than happy, and much more than just me. Thank you, Tim. Thank you, Julie. Thank you, Twentieth-Century Fox.

waiting

The Golden Griddle Pancake House;
First Restaurant Job, 1980 - 1983

"Okay. This is the pantry. And over here is the line. Kitchen. The grills. You know? Have you seen the menu yet? It's like a thesaurus. How many words can you think of to describe a pancake?

"Sometimes you'll drop someone's breakfast on the floor. The floor is pretty clean — most of the time.

"That's Peter over there working the meat grill. He served in 'Nam and when the restaurant gets really busy at lunch on Sunday, he can't handle it. He, like, starts to make coleslaw. Then he has to go home. Usually we don't even need the coleslaw.

"That's the owner's daughter, Leanne. She's a little bit slow, but she needed the job because her special school's out for the summer and her mother is too strung out on Valium to watch over her. Her brother jerks off all the time and sometimes hides inside the cleaning cupboard. Uh-huh. Andy. He works here, too.

"Sometimes we have to deep-fry our bacon because we're so busy and Peter is either shredding cabbage or being driven home by Randy. Randy is the assistant

supervisor. He talks like a girl. I heard that he has a problem with his throat, but I just think he's gay. But don't say
that. If Debbie hears you say gay or fag she'll fire you in a
flash. Debbie is our supervisor, she's Randy's sister, but
you met her in the interview, didn't you? She's the only
one allowed to make the fruit compotes because nobody
else knows how to handle the glucose. She smokes a lot
and has been married twice.

"Peter and I are the only white people that work the
line at night. Except for Fred, but he's in a rock band and
doesn't work much in the summer because of rehearsals.
Their sound is like Journey meets Olivia Newton-John.
So nighttime in the summer means you're going to be
working with either Doug or Dale or Peter or me or Mike.

"Dale is older and very smart. He has a great car with
an amp in the trunk that pumps the bass up on his stereo.
Sometimes when he drives by you'd think you were in an
earthquake. He's taught me all about reggae and funk and
Bob Marley and to appreciate bass. He says my soul is black.
I can rollerskate.

"Mike — he's the one that's not here, the one with the
big eyes. He's tall and thin and is supposed to become a
famous athlete. He fucked my friend Mona. It was her
first time and she fell in love with him. It wasn't his first
time, though. I don't think they're going to get married.

"Doug's in the back having a smoke. You probably saw
him when you punched your timecard. Did you punch
in? Yeah. Doug's my best friend. We have the same birthday. We even smoke the same cigarettes. Cool, eh? He's
the only one who works here who looks good in the

uniform. Yeah, don't you just love the black-and-white checked polyester pants? Some day these are going to become huge sellers in the fashion industry. Hmmm? I'm 16. How old are you? Oh. Is this your first job? Oh, then welcome to hell. This is my first job, too. I swear I'll never work in another restaurant again as long as I live."

Bemelmans;
17th Restaurant Job, 1991 - 1993

I serve lunch to escorted women with thick makeup over their sunburnt, wrinkled skin. They talk in loud, New York-accented voices about Central Park West and their poor, dear friends who can't afford to live there, God love them, and they wonder why I bring their appetizers before their meals. They tell me to hurry up in voices so loud I'm afraid the waiters at the restaurant next door can hear them. They tell the busboy I am rude.

He nods and says, "Coffee?"

When the women have finished showing off their newest piece of jewellery (the husband got a blowjob) and there is nothing left to talk or complain about (except me), they turn to the meals that have been sitting in front of them for ten minutes. Not surprisingly, the food is now cold and, of course, I am to blame. I bring the food back to the kitchen, it gets microwaved, and I bring it out again.

"Mmmm. This is much better."

They swill wine, from labels they cannot pronounce, drain lipstick-smeared glasses, click press-on nails against

the marble tabletops, and smirk as I serve the people beside them. Bits of food and sauce collect at the corners of
their mouths and fly forward when they speak. It's like
watching Tammy Bakker clones doing bad impressions of
Linda Blair in *The Exorcist*. I smoke cigarettes in the back to
shake my anger.

On their way out the door the women ignore me.
Their husbands thank me politely, eyes lowered, and leave
me an outrageously large tip. I almost feel sorry for them,
but I don't pity people who are boorish, or those who
keep them company. I do not slander these strange coup-
lings as do some of the other waiters. I know that their
behavior has nothing to do with race or religion, despite
popular and persistent stereotypes. Perhaps I empathize
with them, for I know too well how stressful it is to per-
petuate a stereotype. It's much bigger than they are.

If you can read between the lines of a waiter's job
description, you will find that we fetch, butt-lick and act
subservient far more than we actually wait. The bourgeois
flash gold cards and condescend to us as temporary help.
The secretaries are too busy to notice us, for they are con-
stantly in a hurry to get separate glasses of water, teabags,
checks, and get back to work. A pocket calculator helps
tally an exact ten percent tip, usually in coin. Waiters are
only appreciated by their own kind, like members of a
secret club, participants in a sacred ritual.

So here I am, stuck in the ghost of a 1980s hotspot,
where the bartender sells more coke than vodka, where
cockroaches stage daily protest marches, and, in the
summer, the entertainment is a live sex show performed

by mice on the back patio.

I vow, here and now, that I'll never work in another restaurant as long as I live.

The Academy;
Last Waiting Job, 1996 – present

"Hi, what can I get for you? Yes, we have beer. What kind of beer would you like? We have about four-dozen kinds. What kind of beer do you usually drink? Coors Lite. Sorry, we don't carry it. We've got Blue Light, Carlsberg Light, Canadian Light, Upper Canada Light Lager, Sleeman Cream Ale, and, on tap, we have Upper Canada Lager, which is fairly light.

"What else? Look, do you see the eighty or so people crowding behind you? Do you see the waitresses glaring at us? Can you see the list of drinks I have to make for the other hundred and twenty-nine people you arrived with by motor coach? You see, you're not helping speed the process along here.

"Something Canadian, then! Alright, a Canadian! Another satisfied customer."

I used to think that you couldn't call yourself a writer or an actress or a singer unless you actually made money doing it. If you paid your bills working as a waiter, then that's what you were. A waiter. Well, I'm not in my twenties anymore. I've had two mothers, countless father figures and one – one – relationship that's lasted longer

than your average television mini-series. I've had friends
come and go and die and come back and get lost. I've had
so many different things happen to me, but one thing has
always stayed the same: I'm always waiting on people.

"Hi. Evelyn? Oh, you're the party organizer. It's nice to
meet you. I've heard so much about you. You find the
nachos a little salty and you'd like a hundred and thirty
glasses of water passed around to all the guests. Well,
Evelyn, that's ... absolutely impossible. You see, we don't
have a sink. That's right. No sink. The owner bought a
grand piano last week, but I'm afraid that a sink didn't fit
into the budget this year. No, that's not sarcasm, Evelyn.
It's frustration.

  "You see, I'm short for rent next month, and I need
a new pair of shoes, and I'm almost out of pot, and I'd
really like to move out of my bachelor apartment and into
a place where I can, you know, entertain and I'm thirty-
four and I've been doing this for sixteen years, Evelyn,
and I've had to deal with so many stuffy, condescending,
anal-retentive, rude, uncultured people that you'd think
... You'd think I'd, uh, be happy to ... One-hundred-
and-thirty glasses of water. Sold to Evelyn the party
organizer in the gabardine pantsuit and colour-coded
name tag. I hope your party is a success.

I've been a waiter, a host, a cook, a dishwasher, a supervisor, an assistant chef and now, finally, a bartender, and
I swear to God this is the last restaurant job I'll ever do.

bruising

This is our secret.

I saw you hanging out the car window, heard your voice slurred by alcohol – beer, probably. People your age either can't afford hard liquor or haven't developed a taste for it. Anyway, I heard you and that made me turn around.

I saw your stringy hair, parted in the middle, the bangs blowing in your face. You had one arm hanging out the window. I could see your long fingers. I pulled my shopping bag close to me, jammed my free hand into my coat pocket. At that moment, I knew I was bound to you for the rest of my life.

It's been a while. I grew a beard, shaved it off, tried a goatee, then remembered how tired that look is. Can't we find another reason to stare at ourselves in the mirror? Shave it off. We should all be bald.

People have told me I've changed since then. Some of my friends have fallen away. Some can't believe I survived it. Others won't speak about it. I know some people can't handle the truth. It doesn't change what I know. My best friend, Murray, said I had no business fucking a straight guy. He told me I was lucky I didn't wind up dead, or in jail. When he stopped calling me I thought about how much things had changed. Was I lucky because of what happened? Murray said I'd developed an edge. He didn't like it. It frightened him. He didn't like the goatee either. How many times I've wanted to ask him if he's ever fucked a stranger, if he's ever hit someone. Have you ever been provoked, Murray? Ever been out of control? Ever have blood on your hands?

Secrets are like cancer, only you can't irradiate them, and telling them won't make them disappear. It only strengthens the truth. What do you do to kill a secret?

Late one night, very late, you stared at me as we passed each other a few blocks from my apartment. It was winter, not long after a snowfall. I remember the sound of the wind whipping the bare tree branches looming above us. We were grey shadows, cast upon the white banks flanking the sidewalk. You shook as we moved for shelter behind an old building. I pulled you to me, kissed your neck, fumbled with your pants, pulled them down to your knees and then took you in my mouth. You gasped and moaned and clenched your fists. You pulled me up, said not here, and asked if I lived nearby. When we got to my apartment you ripped your clothes off, your cock bursting with need. As I touched and sucked you, you shuddered, pulled back and forth. Then you stopped me, grabbed my cock awkwardly. I stopped you. You were hurting me. Then you begged me, shaking violently. I did it. And afterward, you cried. I watched you dress quickly and walk out of my apartment.

Do you believe in fate? What would you do differently if you had known? Would you have begged me? Would you have called me in the middle of the night, petrified, confused, worried? Would you have come back to my apartment four more times so I could fuck you again? Are those the actions of a sexually confused man? What made you think I cared if you ran home and cried into your pillow, aching and terrified? I wasn't responsible for that. But you couldn't see it that way. So I became your enemy — not your confusion, not your homosexuality, not your inner voices, not God — your enemy. It became something I did to you. Like rape. But you asked for it and you enjoyed it and then came around for more. But it was still rape because part of you hated what was happening to you. I wish I could be sorry.

What were you thinking when you rounded up your friends, killed the pain with beer and drove around looking for me? Was it revenge for an injustice? Or were you trying to exorcise your demons? You gave me too much power. You gave everything to me. And when you finally found me, how many weeks later, walking up the street with my groceries, I had almost forgotten about you.

I pulled my shopping bag to my side, worried that I might drop it and break the eggs. I stuck my free hand in the pocket of my jacket, I heard your voice, saw your bony fingers, remembered noticing your ravaged fingernails, felt the rush inside that told me to run. The car stopped. Masculine voices roared. No one else thought anything was happening. Nobody stopped to look. You followed me as I ran, leaving your friends behind, waiting for you to show up with bloodied knuckles, something to prove you were one of them, not other, not queer. You chased me past where we first met. Except this time there was no wind or shadows, just heartbeats and sweat, and the threat of blood.

You called out to me as I fumbled with my keys in the lobby of my building. You caught the door just as it was swinging shut.

"What do you want?"

A shrug. A sheepish, confused look on your face. "Let me come in. Just for a minute. Please."

"Why should I?" I asked, heart still racing. "You were gonna beat me up. So what's the problem? You don't think you're gay? Having a hard time dealing with it? Well I can't help you."

Your eyes avoiding mine, you pulled the door back slowly, opening up the space between us.

"I'm sorry," you said. "This has been ..." A quaver, then tears, and your arms opening out for me, an invitation, an opportunity to calm and comfort.

"Alright."

I know what you would have done if you'd caught me on the street, I told you inside my apartment. It's called bashing. And if you get caught, you can go to prison where you might not have any say in who sticks what up your ass.

Inside my apartment, I put the shopping bag down on the floor and moved closer. Your outstretched arms, your face terrified with longing. A step closer, too close, in a millisecond, your fear and hatred rushed forward, a dam breaking. I saw it, but was too late. Your hands wrapped around my throat, closed in tight. I managed a few punches to your face and arms, a few hindered kicks as we wrestled.

"Don't you want me to fuck you now?" I managed to

scream, your hard, suddenly heterosexual hands around my throat. You shifted your weight and threw me to the ground. My knees, my throat, my eyes burned. I was on fire. You circled around me as I started to get up. You stepped on the eggs. I heard them crack. There goes to-morrow's breakfast. I was going to go out and get laid, make some guy breakfast in the morning. I wondered if I'd ever get laid again.

My breakfast plate was there on the floor. The rind of an empty grapefruit and a grapefruit knife. All of the years of names, queer and faggot, became a white-hot molten rock waiting to explode. Did you deserve it? How many times did I stab you? What would you have done to me if that knife hadn't been there? Does it matter?

Do you feel it when I piss on your grave?

If. I can play with this word all day, picking it up, shaping it, molding it until its hint of possibility turns into a reality where love has no sting when another refuses to return it. I would like to make *if* the world we live in so that he would come back and I wouldn't be so afraid.

Like anyone in a thrall, I have made mistakes, done things a clearer eye would see as dangerous or questionable. Such are the consequences of brushing up against people who offer sweet nothings in beautifully wrapped packages. Surprised and impressed, I floated in blissful clouds of ecstasy, convinced that what I was feeling was the most important thing in the world. Thankful for the shiny presents, I poured gasoline all over myself in return, lit a match, and set myself on fire in a brilliant, dazzling display that lasted months. Now, inside my charred shell remains everything I had ignored: Who I am, my wants, my needs, my successes, my failures, my weaknesses, my strengths. In the ashes too is a need to understand why I still care and feel for the man who gave me the initial spark. Like a low tide, he is never out of sight, and no argument is complete or convincing enough to make me understand why it would be less painful to walk away from the experience than to keep surrendering to the forces that keep me bound to the possibility of what might have continued to be. It's not because I have less to lose by leaving, but rather because I have nothing to gain if I stay. But this is not an answer, not an excuse, nor is it enough.

He is free now, having told me to move on. He left me thinking that someone else would certainly come along and fill the void his absence has created, but I was wrong. So despite trying to avoid him, trying not to look at the objects that remind me of him, or to touch the things his hands once held, his memory floods back because his fingerprints are everywhere.

He is beside me and inside me. I can't seem to make that final effort to lose him, so I let him stay, playing *if* games that could inspire a different conclusion, hoping that its hint of possibility turns into a reality.

opportunity

Andrea pulls the covers over her flannel nightgown, comfortable, unrevealing. She doesn't read or pray. She turns off the light and lies there, thinking and wondering, begging for sleep to take her. She listens to the rustle of the autumn wind blowing lifeless leaves from the trees. Who makes these things happen?

The nights Martin stays in the city, she visualizes the picture of him on the dresser across the room in the darkness. Andrea is getting used to the solitude, but still lies awake wondering why she waits for him. She does not miss his touch, but she misses her love for him. Where has it gone?

During Martin's increasingly infrequent visits, he sleeps without touching her. She wonders if he is being held back by the force ingrained in men by the generations before them, the force that tells them women are strange beasts and must be watched carefully. Like pressure cookers, only with breasts and lips and a place inside them for babies to sleep. Andrea wraps herself in silence and blankets and wishes for liquid dreams where there are no closed spaces, no separations. No solitude.

Occasionally, when Martin wants her, he will leave the light on in the closet and get undressed, stroking himself, arousing himself. How can she resist him? She doesn't think she can. She is his wife. She made the vows. To have and to hold. She submits. But her weakness bears a resentment like a child. Another child.

He exhales deeply, catching a tuft of her auburn hair. The muscles in his thighs contract as he thrusts, oblivious to her silence, her unfocused eyes. She wonders where he goes when he's not with her, where he is when he's on top and inside her. Even in lovemaking he is an illusion, seemingly close, his eyes shut, lips smiling. He's bemused, she thinks beneath him, inside me.

With half-open eyes, he pulls out and nuzzles his head into the pillow on the other side of the bed, forgetting a goodnight kiss. Soon he will be gone.

This night, Andrea feels something approaching above the rustling of the leaves. There's a void growing inside her. She accepts it in the same way she acquiesces to Martin's excuses and sudden plans, forgotten engagements, long working hours, and nights spent in the city. She can accept almost anything.

Andrea is only vaguely aware of Martin's body lying at her side under the peaches-and-cream duvet cover, between layers of matching sheets. She regards the wooden shafts of the four-poster bed that frames the two of them. Tonight they seem too close

She stares up at the white lining of the canopy looming above, like the God she was forced to imagine by parents and pious men in black suits, the God she abandoned in Sunday School. (If God is a man then he must have a thing. How big is it?) Andrea could run faster than any boy at school. She had the highest marks. She didn't hide what she could do, and decided she would not buy into this God business, thank you very much. But then, maybe it was the other way around. Maybe God had abandoned her by not making himself real to her. She needed to see Him. She needed proof.

"Faith," the priests would say, "is what makes God real."

Well then, she thought, what is faith? Faith was not enough. Believing was for people who were too frightened to know things. And Andrea wanted to know many things.

Where do babies come from? What's a war? When is daddy coming home? Why is mommy always so sad? A five-year-old's questions. She could not ask them then. Andrea would not know the answers until much later — well after her mother had slid into a muted, delicate madness from which she would never return.

A dull ache spreads between her legs, accompanied by a prickly pin-stabbing. It's new to her. It spreads through her body. She shudders and shuts her eyes, closing off the heavens above. God would wait for her eyes to open again. God would wait. So they had told her.

A trace of semen trickles slowly down her thigh. Or is it perspiration?

She remembers the morning two weeks ago when she dashed from the bed to the bathroom where, hunched over the toilet, she vomited violently, repeatedly. This happened three days in a row. Martin had slept through two of these incidents and wasn't there for the third. She didn't tell him what she thought it meant. And when she brought the pregnancy test home from the drug store and it turned the alarming colour, she didn't tell him that either. Martin would have to wait.

"Marty," she whispers into the dark. "Marty, are you seeing someone?"

There is no response except for the chirping of a cricket outside. Marty is far away, asleep, with Andrea awake beside him, praying for life to dump a burden on her that she could embrace and struggle with, something concrete and unnerving, something catastrophic. Just something.

Her arms beside her, her body arching slightly with the rise and fall of her breathing, Andrea sleeps, caught in a recurring dream where she is in a gleaming metallic elevator that is ascending very slowly, creating a slight pull in her stomach, which is full and round. She is alone with a man operating the elevator. He is old, with piercing blue eyes and a deep-blue uniform with gold buttons. Andrea sees him looking at her and becomes conscious of her pregnant stomach and puffy, glowing skin. She senses the weight of his stare, feels his body pressing up against her own, but he stands several yards away, his eyes seeing past her, through her. She doesn't know which reality to trust. Panic.

"Why is it taking so long?" Her voice sounds distorted, like it's under water.

He responds with an evasive smile. She folds her hands in front of her belly and watches as the numbers on the panel slowly light up and then darken.

The elevator stops, ending the pull in her stomach. The doors slide open.

Andrea opens her eyes and sits up in bed. Fractured

images from the dream race through her consciousness, escaping comprehension. The room around her is black. She feels sharp splinters of pain. She pats some sweat off her forehead and glances at the clock on the table to her left. 3:17.

She turns to see if she's disturbed Martin, but the space beside her is empty. She reaches her hand out and feels no warmth from the creases he has left in the sheets.

Rising from the bed and covering her nightgown with a thin, frilly house robe, Andrea makes her way to the bedroom door. She opens it and calls out Martin's name twice, but gets no response. Before going downstairs, Andrea stops for a moment, chasing away thoughts of prowlers. She's never worried about intruders before. Funny.

The kitchen is dark and empty. She moves further along the hallway to the den. With a twist of her wrist and a gentle thrust, the door opens to a room lined with photographs and sketches.

She sits down on the piano bench and switches on a small lamp that throws an uneasy light on the space. Andrea pulls her robe evenly around her legs. She glances up and looks at the pictures arranged on top of the piano. There is a small snapshot of her and Martin camping in Algonquin Park, when Martin almost fainted after being stung by a bee. To the left of it is a portrait of Andrea and her mother taken many years ago at the nursing home.

Her mother is looking off to the side, teeth clenched. Andrea's hands are resting, or rather, placed on her mother's shoulders. Andrea looks as if she is trying to appear assertive, in control. Her mother's eyes appear lost, beyond reach.

In the centre of the arrangement of photographs is a large, brass-framed wedding picture. Andrea looks at the faces of the couple in the picture and can barely recognize their expressions. She remembers the weather that day, warm and breezy. It was a perfect summer wedding. "I do," she had said. She did. Now she wishes it had rained.

She rises and goes to the window and looks outside into the still, dark night and a word bubbles up before she has a chance to suppress it.

Opportunity.

Diffuse light whispers into the bedroom through cold-frosted windows. The harsh, tinny alarm clock stings Andrea out of her sleep. She reaches out to adjust the volume, but misses the knob and knocks the clock to the carpeted floor. The alarm is silenced. Andrea sits up, notices the nightstand is too close to the bed, pushes it back several inches, then replaces the clock on top of it. The digital display is dark. She looks down at the electrical outlet. The alarm clock has come unplugged. Andrea ignores it and settles back under the covers, noticing the sound of the shower running. Within moments, the water stops and small noises come from the bathroom.

She hears Martin go to the closet. She peers out from her shelter and catches a glimpse of his buttocks, dotted with water. He rubs a towel into his slick hair and then throws it onto the closet floor. He pulls on a pair of white underwear — shorts Andrea washes every week — and then turns around. She stifles a gasp as she notices a small purplish spot at the base of Martin's neck. A hickie?

Opportunity.

Andrea lies still until he has left. Only then does she rise to make coffee. But there are no beans, so she makes tea instead, and drinks it slowly, indifferently. She has no milk. The hot, bitter liquid trickles down her throat.

Her day dissolves into a series of disconnected movements. Objects around her seem to be either too close or too far away. She worries, while washing dishes, that her hands are unsteady and she's about to break a plate or teacup. The strokes she makes with her arms while vacuuming seem out of alignment. Her legs move spasmodically. Something has thrown her mechanism askew.

After vacuuming, Andrea spends an hour pushing all the furniture in the living room back against walls, rearranging it, making more room. She feels a light pressure on her, as if the outside world is reaching down and inward but can't seem to synchronize with her innards. She feels a tightness in her chest and stomach as if her heart were a looffah scrubbing away at her insides. Maybe it's just the pregnancy. Just the baby.

She stops for a few minutes to drink some water and nibble at a half-baked cookie from a failed batch she made several days before. Perhaps she forgot to put something in the batter. Eggs. Probably eggs.

She decides to postpone dusting the corners of the ceiling until she feels more stable standing on a chair.

Instead, she removes all the statues and doilies from the living room mantle and tables and dusts there. Sometime after lunch Andrea falls asleep amid pillows in a chair in the living room, sliding imperceptibly into a dream of a small room that contains only a small cot and a telephone. She sits on the cot and repeatedly picks up the receiver and dials her mother's number. After a few moments she hangs up. She knows that her mother is home, but why isn't she answering? Although she doesn't live far away, Andrea has been too busy to visit; so the only way that the two can communicate is by telephone. She must speak to her. Andrea leaves the room and goes to check to make sure she's alright. She arrives at a tall building that rises so high she can't see the top.

The moment she steps into the building, she's in an elevator whizzing upwards at incredible speed. There is an old man with brilliant-blue eyes operating it. The device stops and the doors swish open. Walking away, she hears the gurgling shrieks of a baby behind her. She turns to look back at the old man and discovers that he is gone, and, in his place, a newborn infant lies on the elevator floor, glistening with blood and crying savagely. Andrea steps toward the elevator to retrieve the child, but her footsteps lead nowhere. She walks faster but just gets further away. The elevator doors close. A trail of blood leads from the elevator to beneath her feet. She looks down and notices a bloodstain on the front of her dress, her suddenly flat stomach, the prickling pain spreading inside her. *Drip, drip.*

Andrea wakes with a gasp and rises abruptly from the

chair. Pillows fall to the floor. She raises her cuff to her
forehead, dabs at the sweat, then looks down at her
stomach. It looks normal. She kicks the pillows out of her
way and moves to the kitchen. Peering inside the fridge,
she wonders what to make for dinner, but then stops
herself. It occurs to her that Marty won't be home for
dinner.

Opportunity.

The telephone rings, startling her. It's Martin, calling
from his office to inform her that he won't be home for
supper. Andrea hangs up without responding.

Andrea steps up onto the doorstep carefully, admiring
her neighbours' ornate mailbox. She presses the door-
bell, squinting at the sun's reflection in the glass door.

Melissa Webber's face appears behind the inner door
she pulls open slowly, astonished that Andrea is standing
there in a bathing suit. Melissa unlocks the glass door and
swings it open.

"Isn't it a little cold for swimming, Andrea?"

"I just need to borrow some molasses, Melissa."

The woman gives Andrea a befuddled look. "I'll see if
I have some. Be right back."

When Melissa returns with a glass jar, Andrea smiles
and reaches for it. "That's wonderful, Mel. Thank you so
much."

Melissa steps outside, watches Andrea crossing the
lawns to her house. As she is about to close the door,

Melissa sees Andrea stop on her driveway, raise the jar above her head, and throw it onto the asphalt. The jar lands with a muted crash. Melissa steps out on her stoop. "Andrea, is everything okay?"

Andrea turns, waves to Melissa, and disappears into the house.

The next evening the phone rings at six. Andrea rises from the recliner in the living room to pick up the receiver on the fourth ring.

"Hello?"

"It's Marty."

"Hello, husband."

"Andrea, I'm sorry to have to do this, but I've got to work late again tonight."

"Oh."

"We've just taken on a new client and Burns is being very careful about their first campaign with us, you know what I mean."

"Yes, I'm sure I do. Martin?"

"Yeah?"

"There's broken glass on the driveway. Be careful you don't cut yourself on it in the dark."

"Broken glass?"

"Yes, broken glass."

"Oh."

"You didn't come home last night."

"No I didn't. And I won't be coming home tonight.

I've got too much work to do, and you know how that drive home kills me late at night."

"Where are you calling from?"

"Work, honey."

"Molasses."

"Huh?"

"On the driveway."

"What?"

"I broke a jar of molasses on the driveway. That's all"

"Oh, I see. Okay, I've got to get to work now. Are you feeling alright? You sound a little funny."

"Then we should both be laughing."

"At what?"

"Huh? I sound funny? That's funny, I don't feel funny. You go to work now, dear." Andrea places the receiver back in its cradle.

The elevator is waiting for her again. The old man with brilliant blue eyes looks patiently at her swollen stomach. Once she's inside he presses the top button and the doors close. Andrea can feel the tug on her stomach, the slight pulling. She wonders if the baby can feel it, too. Her eyes dart between the old man and the flashing numbers on the panel.

They come to a halt. The doors open. Andrea steps into an endless grey room filled with hundreds of metal tables lit by harsh fluorescent lighting. *Drip, drip.* On each table sits a large beaker filled with a deep-red liquid.

From the ceiling hang hundreds of naked female bodies, suspended from their necks by thick rope. *Drip, drip.* A scream rattles out of Andrea's throat and ends with a sudden gasp. A chill freezes her as she stares into the dead eyes of the body suspended just a few feet away, its skin pale grey and rotting. A trail of blood trickles from between its legs, into the beaker. *Drip, drip.*

Andrea sees her own eyes bulging out of the lifeless face. She steps forward, focuses on the next cadaver and sees her face again. It's her, they're all her. She pulls back, gasping for air. Another scream bounces off the shiny metal tables. It echoes and stabs her ears like the sound of babies dying.

"I think it's time we sat down and had a talk," Martin says, falling into the blue-and-green striped chair in the living room. He crosses one leg over the other.

Andrea watches as the cuffs of his pants ride up around his ankles. Black socks with gold paisleys. She moves her glance upward, focusing on the hair on Martin's knuckles, thinking about his long, thick fingers.

"Andrea, honey? Are you listening to me?"

"Yes, Marty. What's wrong?"

"That's what I'd like to talk about. Finally. It, uh, it's a difficult thing to talk about, but I know we should."

"What's on your mind?"

Martin uncrosses his legs and leans forward, cupping his chin in his right hand. If he still smoked, surely he would be lighting up right now. Andrea remembers his overflowing ashtrays and the cigarette burns on the furniture she tried to conceal with pillows, afghans, and doilies. Such frivolous decorations had never appealed to her until she needed them to cover up Martin's mistakes. It was a difficult time. Martin's problems, his tantrums, his indifference, brooding into the night. The silence. Sometimes she thought she would go crazy from not knowing. And now, a tiny voice in her titters that things have indeed turned around. Now it is Martin who is worried.

Andrea's mouth twitches. A pain in her abdomen. She readjusts her weight, moves from against the wall and into a chair facing Martin. He doesn't notice her discomfort. Perhaps he's used to it.

"I think we should talk about spending some time apart. I've been working a lot lately and spending more time than I should at the office. And I've met someone."

"You fucker," Andrea says, not unpleasantly.

"Andrea, I need you to listen to me on this."

"Sure, dear," she says, folding her hands on her lap. "I'm all ears." Her tone startles him. He moves his right hand to the arm of the chair. His left hand moves to one of his shirt buttons. He fiddles with it. Andrea watches his fingers at the button. Remembering them, feeling something – what? – a moistness seeping through. Those long fingers once made her wet. She squirms at the memory, erotic and unsettling.

Oppor - tunity.

A stabbing pain. Andrea brings her hands to her stomach, as if shielding an impending blow. Martin notices her grimace.

"What is it?"

"Nothing. What do you want to say? You've met some-body. So now what? A divorce? Separation?"

Oppor - tunity.

"Are you sure you're alright?" He comes over to kneel down in front of her. She wants to hit him.

"Tell me!" she demands, pushing him away. Martin lurches backwards, regarding Andrea as a doctor would a patient displaying a mysterious affliction.

She gets up and walks past him. He is about to follow her, but something pulls his eyes to the chair. A mark. A stain? In red. He turns to Andrea and sees a red blotch on her dress.

"Andrea …"

Slowly she follows his eyes and looks down at the yel-low pleats. She spies the stain, feels something, utters a sound. Martin is behind her as she crumples. He catches her and eases her onto the floor. He runs to the phone and dials 911, shouting his name and address into the receiver.

When he goes back to her, Andrea has curled up in the fetal position, hugging her legs. Martin bends down and brushes some hair out of her eyes and whispers her name softly into her ears, tells her that everything is going to be alright, everything is going to be fine. "I'm sorry, honey, don't worry, everything is going to be alright, every-thing is going to be fine."

The ambulance backs over the mess of broken glass and molasses. The paramedics don't notice it and move quickly inside the house with their bags at their sides. When they reach Andrea, her breathing has become shallow, her face pale and ghostly. Martin is sitting beside her with a glass of scotch in his hand, a desperate look on his face.

"Mr. Montgomery?" one of the paramedics asks, staring at Martin's chest.

"Yes. What's wrong with her?"

"It's a bit early to be sure," one paramedic says evenly as he removes instruments from his case.

Martin nurses his scotch as the two men hover over his wife, checking her pulse, heart-rate, blood pressure.

"Does your wife take any medicaton?"

"No. Just aspirin for the occasional headache, I sup- pose. Vitamins. Calcium?" He gets up and moves to the liquor cabinet in the kitchen to refill his glass. When he returns, the paramedics have pulled Andrea's dress up to her thighs. Martin regards them with detached curiosity.

After a prolonged silence, the paramedics sit up from inspecting Andrea and give each other a grim nod. One man stands up, pulls a cell phone from his belt and goes outside. The other readjusts Andrea's dress.

"Is your wife pregnant, Mr. Montgomery?"

"I don't know."

"There's internal bleeding. We're going to have to take her in."

"Do you know what's causing it?"

"Not at this point. We need to get her to the hospital."

She rises from the hospital bed and moves toward the door. The intravenous tubing pulls taut as she walks away. She feels a tug on her arm and then a slackness as the needle pops out and falls to the ground. She passes through the hallway, past the nurses' station, unnoticed. She pushes the up button for the elevator and waits until its red light goes dark. Voices swirl in and out of her consciousness like a radio flying back and forth across the dial. The elevator door opens. She steps inside.

There is an old man with gleaming blue eyes in the elevator. He regards her and nods his head. His mouth has been sewn shut. There is desperation in his eyes. She looks at the panel in front of her, presses a button near the top, a button without a number, and feels the pull in her stomach.

The elevator ride seems endless. Several times Andrea glances over at the silent man to find him staring glumly back at her. Finally the elevator slows and stops. The doors open and Andrea steps out into a large, reverberant room. It is a familiar room, filled with bodies. She notices the ropes circling their necks, suspending them.

Opportunity.

She steps forward, focusing on the face closest to her. She's looking into a mirror, into the future, into her own dead face. She follows the rotting down to the tiny rivulets of blood trickling out of the vagina, landing in the beaker with a hollow drop that, with ten-thousand simultaneous drops, echoes through the room. The sound pierces her ears like the blade of a knife. She stumbles, almost falls.

Opport-unity.

A muffled grunt echoes through the room. Andrea composes herself, takes a few steps forward, trying not to touch the bodies, hesitates, then looks back, but she's so far into the space now that she can barely see the elevator. Another sound penetrates her ears. She spins around and sees a hazy figure in the distance. As she advances toward the figure, the sound of breathing, frantic whispers, and low moaning intensifies.

She looks around her and remembers the gleaming metallic tables, the jars of red and the thousands of dead dripping bodies suspended above the tables. And her face on every one of the bodies, a noose around her neck. And the single word whispered in her ears like a warning, or a prayer: *Opport - unity*, the slight break after the second syllable. But as she looks around the same room, there are no tables, no blood-filled glass jars, no bodies, not even her face. They are all behind her. She stops.

She sees a large operating table. On it are two figures intertwined, naked, it seems, writhing, making ecstatic, sexual sounds. Andrea strains her eyes but she can only make out bits and pieces of body parts; a section of one figure's back, a thick calf, an armpit, a curved neck, and fingers, with dark hair on the knuckles.

Something clicks inside her. She almost feels it. Like knowledge.

Abort unity.

She turns and moves back toward the elevator. The vast room is empty. Andrea quickens her pace. As she approaches the elevator, she hears the sound of a faint heartbeat growing louder and slower. She stops at the elevator doors. Pushes the down button. The doors slide open. Andrea sees a smiling, radiant child inside, and steps in. The doors close. The dream fades.

When she wakes up, Andrea hears the hum of male voices in the room. Through blurred vision, a figure pulls apart into two, and one leaves the room. Moments later another figure enters and approaches her. A man's voice speaks to her, asks questions, explains something, tells her to rest. "You'll be fine, Mrs. Montgomery, just fine," the voice says.

Andrea rolls her head to the side and closes her eyes. She tries to sleep, but cannot. Martin speaks to her, re-iterates what the doctor said, that she'll be fine. Just fine. But that isn't enough. She wants out, out of the bed, out of the room and hospital. She wants to go back to the ele-vator in the dream and hold the smiling baby. She feels the needle pumping her with God and light and plastic, the tape on her arm holding the IV in place. She feels the light sheets on top of her, a numbness between her legs, an emptiness in her stomach, and the wedding ring around her finger.

the guy next door

i don't know much about the guy next door except for what I've heard late at night when the walls between our apartments are at their thinnest. I hear music, sometimes just a rhythmic thumping, sometimes a melody. Saturday mornings he plays Nina Simone or Miles Davis. Sometimes both. Sunday nights I hear television laughter.

A few weeks ago, he had a party and played Anita O'Day and Mel Tormé into the wee hours. I sat up in my bed with my ear against the wall, listening for information; a name, a place of business, a favourite hangout, but I couldn't make anything out from the hum of party guests.

One Friday night I carry my soiled clothing and detergent to the basement to do laundry. I push open the laundry room door and turn the corner toward the washers. There, sitting on the folding counter, listening to a Walkman is an attractive thirty-fivish man with dark hair. He nods. I smile back.

Once the wash cycles have commenced, I sit down atop one of the machines and pull Carrie Fisher's *Surrender The Pink* out of my laundry bag.

"I've heard about that book. Is it good?"

I put it down and smile. "Excellent. This is my third read."

"Oh really? It must be good, then."

"She's one of my favourite writers."

"My name is David."

"Hi David," I say, looking directly at him in the harsh fluorescent light.

"You live in the building?"

I chuckle. "Yes I do."

"Oh, well, I thought you might be, you know, visiting someone here. I was just wondering, that's all."

"My name is Brian."

"Nice to meet you, Brian. Are you single?"

Again, I laugh. "Uh, yeah."

"Are you gay?"

"Yes I am. You don't have a questionnaire with you, do you?"

"Just wondering," he says with a smile, shrugging.

"Okay."

"In case you're not busy one night. Or are you not the dating type?"

I smile, embarrassed. "Yes, I'm the dating type."

"I didn't mean to offend you."

"Oh, I'm not offended."

He gives a little shrug and looks up at the ceiling.

I pull the book up again and try to resume reading, but I can't concentrate on the words. I know that my eyes are following the words and sentences, but I retain nothing. I'm thinking about this man sitting across from me, of restarting the conversation, but he's put his Walkman on again. I glance at my watch. Only five minutes have passed since the machines started up. This could very well become the longest Friday night of my life.

Later, after I've folded and ironed everything, I take the book to bed, and hope to hear some signs of life from next door. I read for half an hour before falling asleep.

I am awakened by a low-pitched growl. My clock shows it's just past two a.m. Moments later I hear a masculine gasp, then a moan accompanied by a loud "Oh, yeah!"

I light a candle and, with my ear against the wall, start stroking myself under the covers. The sex lasts for almost two hours. By the time it's over, I've gone through half a bottle of lube, two towels, and am aching to get to sleep.

As I'm about to drift off, I hear two voices arguing, then a door being slammed. The guy next door is now probably alone. I fall asleep trying to create a face, a body, a name, but all I come up with is a huge cock.

I decide that having a party might be a good way to meet my neighbour. Just as soon as I buy some nice furniture. This might take some time.

I bump into David from the laundry room going down on the elevator one day. He removes his Walkman's earplugs. "I'm sorry ... I don't remember your name."

"It's Brian."

"How's it going?"

"Oh, fine. How about you?"

"Okay. What floor do you live on, Brian?"

"I live on the fourteenth floor."

"Oh really? You mean the thinly disguised thirteenth floor."

"Uh-huh. 1412."

"Hmmm. 1412." One eyebrow goes up and then he

quickly looks away.

This guy is a bit weird, I think. Maybe he's just nervous. His dark hair is combed back over his head. He looks incredibly sexy. He looks as though he might have hair on his back. Maybe he gets it waxed? He's wearing tight black jeans, black cowboy boots, a black biker jacket and carrying a black gym bag. Hmmmm. Ditch the cowboy boots, though.

"Going to work out?" I ask.

"No," he says, shifting his weight. "Going to see a friend in the hospital."

"Oh. AIDS?"

"No. Breast cancer."

"Oh. Sorry to hear that."

Silence.

Ground floor.

"You going to be in later tonight?"

I shrug. "I'm not sure. Why?"

"I thought I might drop by. You know, maybe we could talk. Or something ..."

"Well, right now I'm not sure what's going on. I'm working until about eight-thirty, or so."

"Oh, well that's okay. I probably won't be back until ten."

By now, we're about to leave the building. I figure, what the hell? He obviously likes me.

"I should be home around nine-thirty. We could have coffee or watch a movie."

"Do you play Monopoly?"

"I haven't played Monopoly in years," I say, surprised.

"Oh, okay. 1412?"

"Yeah, see you. Hope your friend's alright."

"She isn't. Bye."

I buy condoms, lubricant and an enema kit. I should change my name to Justin Case. Because chances are, with my track record, David will show up with a Monopoly game tucked under his arm and a bottle of Diet Coke. "Can't we just cuddle?" he'll ask, not wanting to take off his clothes.

It's the tease syndrome. Men act like they really, really like you and would stop at nothing – not even board games – to get you hooked on them. Then, once they see that you are, they become indifferent. "Oh, I have to go to my apartment to watch 90210. See you later." I know the strategy well. I don't take it personally. Not any more. They leave me with incense and candles and a burning hard-on. I don't have sex with my dates anymore. As soon as they see I'm interested in them, they leave. Sometimes we just skip right past the first date and break up after we're introduced. It saves tears. Tears and time. It's a sign of my times.

My drugstore outing sets me back twenty-four dollars and ninety-six cents. On my way home, a young guy in baggy clothes and spiked hair stops me on the sidewalk and asks me for change. I reach in my pocket and pull out four pennies. It's all I have. His eyes grow wide when he sees what I've deposited in his hand. Then he looks angry and throws the pennies at my feet as I walk away.

David arrives at my door shortly after ten with a Monopoly board under his arm. "Ready to play?"

I put on some Miles Davis. *Kind Of Blue*. David smiles

when the first chords sound.

"Oh, I love Miles Davis. I listen to this CD in the mornings on weekends with my lover when we have our coffee."

"You have a lover?"

"Well, yeah ... a boyfriend. Kind of." David turns to me with a serious look on his face. "That's what I want to talk to you about. I don't really know you from a hole in the wall, but I need to talk to someone. Do you mind?"

"No," I answer, wondering why doesn't he talk to his friends. "What's the matter?"

He looks away suddenly, toward my room. "Could you turn off the music and come in the bedroom with me?" He practically jumps out of his chair and runs to the bedroom door.

I rush to turn off the stereo and then make my way to the bedroom. When I enter it, David is already on the bed, lying on his stomach with his ear to the wall.

"What are you doing?"

"Ssshh!" He waves his hand at me.

Then I hear it. A low-pitched groan. "No! Please! Fuck me. Fuck me! Oh yeah!"

At first it sounds like a porno, but then something or someone slams against the wall. David sits up and leans against the wall, almost knocking my Kate Bush picture-disc-clock off the wall. I know I hung it too low ...

"What are you doing?" I ask again. He's shielding his eyes with his right hand. Before I know it he starts sobbing.

"I'm sorry. I ... That's my boyfriend in there. Fucking bastard."

"Really? Are you sure?"

"Yes."

"Oh, I'm sorry."

"Brian, you're a nice guy. I didn't do this ... Shit!" He sits at the edge of the bed and stares at the floor for a moment before continuing. "I thought he was fucking around on me."

"Why don't you go and confront him?"

"It's not my apartment."

"You mean you don't live with him?"

"No. I live on the seventeenth floor."

"I've always wondered who I was listening to over there," I say. "Even fantasized about him."

David wipes his eyes and moves toward me on his hands and knees.

"I thought maybe I could get revenge by dating somebody else," he says. "Then I met you and thought I'd give it a whirl."

"You thought you'd give me a whirl? Well doesn't that make my day!"

"Hold on a minute." He composes himself a bit, then continues. "But then I kind of started to like you and ... he's been getting a little rough in bed and ... I just thought it was time to bail out. Well, I know I'm going to have to end it now."

There's an uncomfortable silence, interrupted by a muffled groan from next door. Our eyes meet.

"End it with me," I say.

"What?"

"Kiss me," I tell him, moving toward him.

He looks at me, puzzled, surprised.

"Kiss me," I say again.

"No, I don't think ..."

I lean forward and kiss him lightly on the lips. I put my hands on his shoulders and kiss him again.

"Did you intend to sleep with me?" I ask him.

"I was hoping that we could ... you know, just sleep together, you know?"

"Cuddle?"

I don't intend to let him or any other man get away with this bullshit ever again. "You mean kissing, necking, lying down on the bed together, massaging each other through our clothes — but we won't do anything — and then taking off our shirts and then just our pants — but we'll leave our underwear on. Then the underwear comes off — but we won't do anything! And then we're jerking each other off and then sucking each other off and then we come all over the place and you have to leave because you can't sleep when you're in bed with another man or you just remembered that your aunt Harriet will be calling long distance from Manchester in a few minutes. A few days later I'll call you and set up a date and then, when we're supposed to go out, you'll cancel because you have to watch *Bewitched* or 90210. Then you won't return my calls and then ..."

"Wait a minute, wait a minute!" He looks at me, bewildered. "That's not cuddling, that's dating."

We both laugh. He's probably just as uptight as I am, but he broke the mood and got me to stop ranting.

"Sorry," I say. "I guess I'm just a little *verklempt* when it comes to men."

"Lighten up! Start a twelve-step group or something. I'm the one with the problem here."

"Yeah? Well, stop whining about it," I say.

"Look who's whining!" He laughs. "This is crazy."

"It is?"

"Uh-huh, it is." He looks at me thoughtfully, then comes over to me, puts his arms around me and gives me a small kiss on the cheek. "I'd better go. Sorry to put you through this. I think we've both let off a bit too much steam for a first date. And, no, I'm not one of those guys who says let's just cuddle when I really want to gobble your horn."

"Gobble my horn?"

"You never heard that before?"

"No."

"I'm not saying that I don't want to ..."

"Gobble my horn ..."

"Yeah. But I have some things I have to sort out and ..."

"Are you sure?"

"About what? Leaving here or leaving my boy-friend?"

"Both."

"You'd want to sleep with me even if I was still seeing Gord?"

Gord! Gord's his name.

"Perhaps we shouldn't do anything until you're a little more clear about all this, huh?"

I didn't mean to be nice, but I remembered all the crap I've been through with men who play games. Why would I want somebody who isn't sure whether he wants me or not? Maybe because I'm safer if I think that he doesn't really want me.

I never did get to meet Gord. David ended the relationship and soon afterward I saw an older man letting
himself into the apartment. He invited me in, but I
declined. I tell David about this when he visits for a game
of Monopoly. He smiles. "It's wise to not get too close to
your neighbours," he says.

kiss off

don stops by my apartment every morning between 8:12 and 8:17 to kiss me. I always have coffee ready in case he wants to stay for a minute, but that would make him late for work, he says.

"Hi baby," he says as he steps into the apartment, smelling clean and looking the way a lover is supposed to look first thing in the morning as he leaves you. He guides the door closed with his left hand. It clicks shut. He is so handsome, he glows. Everything about him is beautiful. The way he talks – he's got a light, self-effacing tone, as if he doesn't really know or believe what he's saying – the way he steps up to me, raising his right hand and placing it on my shoulder as he leans in for the kiss.

It's not a casual kiss, but he always looks glad afterward, even though I don't know how it makes him feel. After I lock the door behind him, I often wonder what it all means, where it's all going, and where it came from. I don't have many answers, and that's probably because I haven't asked any questions. All I have is the kiss.

A kiss is not an easy thing to describe. The way somebody moves their mouth against yours, touches you with their tongue, presses against you, maybe even breathing a sigh of relief. It's not something you're bound to see a "how to" article about in *Chatelaine* magazine in the grocery checkout line. Some people just know how to do it better than others. Some are born kissers. Others are clumsy and awkward, seem to have no control over their mouths. I like to think that you should be able to communicate any emotion through a kiss.

Two days ago, Don showed up at 8:23. He hadn't shaved.

"I actually slept in," he said with a surprised grin. "Can you believe that?"

"You still came by."

"Sure. I can't miss my kiss."

I kept my eyes open. It was a quick kiss. He moved back slowly and smiled, raising his right arm and touching the side of my face. "You're so beautiful," he said.

I thought perhaps he might kiss me again, telling me all I needed to know with his lips, but he stood still, looking at me.

"What is it?" he asked, caressing my cheek, tilting his head to the side a bit.

I lowered my eyes, wrapped my arm around his waist. "You're beautiful, too, Don." Slight pause. "I, uh ..."

"What? Something wrong?"

"No." I pulled myself into him, close, hugged him, put my face to his neck, my mouth near his ear. "I like that you come here every morning and kiss me."

"I like it too," he said, returning my embrace.

Our first kiss was unexpected. We had met through mutual friends, over drinks at a bar. I excused myself to use the washroom, and when I came out, Don was pretending to use the payphone in the corridor. As I walked toward him, I heard him say, "There's somebody here I have to kiss or I'm going to explode." He hung up and pulled me into him. His arms wrapped around me like they knew every inch of my body. His instinct was uncanny. I felt his breath on my face, his lips lightly touching mine. I opened my mouth.

We broke up two months ago after being together for just over a year. It surprised me when, the next day, he showed up on my doorstep to give me a kiss. The next day he showed up again. And then the day after that.

What commitment is there in a kiss?

brad descending

"There's nothing wrong with you, Brad."

"You're just going to sit there sucking that pencil while I waste away, aren't you?"

"Waste away?"

Finally he agrees.

"I want some drugs!"

Brad stares at the middle-aged doctor seated across the desk in a snug, naugahyde chair.

"Are you just going to sit there, girl?" Brad says. "I mean, I don't know what else you need to know." He closes his eyes, thinking about the scratchiness in his throat, the backache. And his fucking useless assistant. How many does that make this year? Four? Five?"

"Brad, you're not sick. Physically." The doctor tells him to take some time off work, go on a trip, relax, see a psychiatrist, start up on Prozac. Again. And then he slides two business cards across the desk, one for a travel agent, the other for a gay-friendly psychiatrist. Brad dismisses everything with a rush of breath and a quick wave of his hand.

"Are you serious? Oh my God, girl, I can't miss even a day of work. I'm the only one who can run that agency. I've got interviews to arrange, lunches to organize, models to interview, fashion shoots to set up. I'm too busy. I'm too stressed out, Nardo, and I'm too tired to take Prozac. Besides," he says, suddenly smiling, "What's Prozac gonna do for me besides stop me from getting a hard-on? I don't think it matters now anyway. Cal brought home a dildo the size of Mount St. Helens." He clears his throat. An expression of panic shoots across his pale face. "There!" he says, pointing at Dr. Nardo. "Was that a cough? See? Oh, why don't you put me on something? Anything. Some antibiotic? An anti-viral, or, whatever, you know? AZT?"

"How about I put you across my knee and give you a spanking?"

"Oh my God, girl!" Brad shrieks. "I didn't know you were into that! Have you slept with Alan Gorley? I heard she's into that. Apparently she likes getting fisted and pissed on, too. And I heard her lover is a big pedo."

"No, Brad. You're being unbelievably silly."

"Well I think maybe I should go somewhere for a sec-ond opinion. Because, you know, you're just so ... being so difficult with me here. And I don't know why."

Nardo reaches forward and pushes the business cards closer to his patient. Brad swans out of the office.

When he gets back to the agency, Brad looks through his daybooks from the past two years to jot down the dates of his various illnesses, infections and afflictions, to pre-pare a case history. He also collects the results of seventeen HIV tests from the past eight years. Every seven months, Brad would haul himself up the steps to the Hassle Free Clinic and get jabbed by the Chinese nurse in a white lab coat. Once he lied and told the nurse he thought he had gonorrhea. What better place than a VD clinic to get sex? As soon as he removed his pants and underwear, the nurse saw his erection, then sat down on a chair on the other side of the examining room. "Am I supposed to be impressed?"

Brad looked at the man in disbelief.

"There's a bathhouse across the street," he said.

Brad didn't move.

"I think you should leave now."

October, 1989, negative. May, 1990, negative. December, 1990, negative. In April of '91 he met Cal, who was positive. Between 1992 and 1995, negative, all negative. Then, five months ago, he stopped having sex with Cal. Brad hired SpeedyBoyz, a company that sends young men in Speedos to clean apartments, houses and offices.

Hmmm. That's when I started coming home late from work. Buster was cleaning. Had to stay 'til he was done. That's when Cal told me I had bad breath one morning. Why do I remember these things?

Not long after that, Buster moved into the spare bedroom in the basement. Cal didn't seem to mind. Perhaps because he was also having sex with Buster, and in no position to complain about Brad doing it. But Brad wasn't to know about Cal and Buster until Buster came home one afternoon from the doctor's office shrieking and crying. His HIV test had come back positive. It was never asked of Buster if he knew who had infected him, but things were quiet around the house for some time. The test results didn't stop Brad from pushing Buster down rather carelessly on his basement bedroom bed, and going at him.

Buster's test results didn't stop Cal from having sex

with him either. It wasn't long before Buster suggested to
Brad that they should have a threesome. Brad just looked
at him vacantly. "Why would I want to have sex with Cal?"

"He's your lover, isn't he?"

"So? Just suck my dick, Buster. Okay, girl?"

When Brad arrives home from the office, it is well
after 8:00. Cal has already eaten, and is sitting in front
of the television with Buster.

"Did you tape *Springer*?" Brad asks from the kitchen.

Cal follows him into the pantry and gives him a quick
peck on the cheek. "Hi pumpkin," he says.

Brad eases himself away. "Hi pumpkin. No leftovers?"

Cal turns his head toward Buster.

"Oh," Brad groans. "Her again. Is she paying part of
our grocery bill?"

"We talked about this before."

"No, you talked, Cal. I argued, and you won. What
can I make that won't take an hour?"

"Why don't you raid my pantry?"

"Puh-leeze. I'm tired." He turns his head toward the
living room. "Why don't you take the maid downstairs
and fuck her like you normally do?"

"Nice, Brad," Cal says, dejected. "This isn't normal,
you know"

"Oh my god, girl, what are you talking about? Normal.
Don't pretend like this is, you know, my problem, okay?
Because it's not."

Brad searches the cupboards for something in a can.
Buster's voice calls out from the living room. "I got the
times mixed up and taped *Sally* by mistake. The topic is 'I've

Got a Secret.' It's a stripper and a fat guy, a drug dealer and his mother, and a couple in their sixties that cross-dress." Cal looks at Brad. Brad groans.

Cal shakes his head and leaves the pantry. Brad eats pasta in a cream sauce and takes a hot shower before going to bed. His striped nightshirt is hanging on the back of the bathroom door. He puts it on and climbs under the sheets next to Cal.

Brad keeps to his own side of the bed but soon senses Cal stirring and then feels hands on his back. They wrap around him and pull him close. Brad nudges himself away and mumbles, "I'm tired."

"How was your day?" Cal asks.

Full of surprises, Brad would like to say, followed by a swift kick. But he's too afraid. Afraid that one thing would lead to another and he'd end up killing Cal. Instead, he utters "Shitty. It was a bad day, pumpkin." He breathes a sigh of relief.

"I love you," Cal says.

"I love you, too, pumpkin," Brad says, thinking about fabric softener, and, briefly, yellow wax beans. Then fear spreads like a chill. What if Cal really means it? Brad never figured this into his plan. Oh, God. What if Nardo was right? No, no. He's wrong. What if Cal really does love me? What if he didn't infect me? Who was it, then? I've never been with anyone else since we started dating. Except Buster and a few guys when Cal was away ... How could this happen? I've never been promiscuous, no more than a hundred lovers or so, most of them safe ... I think.

Before long, Cal is asleep. Brad turns onto his back

and stares up at the ceiling. The anger surfaces again and he can't bear to be beside Cal a moment longer, so he retreats to the spare bedroom and traces imaginary drawings in the irregular patterns of the stucco ceiling. As his eyes grow heavy, he begins to see slivers of dim light creeping through the blinds. They seem to be reaching toward him, but he drifts off before they can touch him.

He wakes to the smell of coffee and Lagerfeld cologne. Cal has already dressed and left for work. Was I dreaming or was that him kissing me on the forehead before he left?

Brad cooks up some eggs and a few slices of toast for breakfast, sipping black coffee. Thinking about nothing in particular, he eats his meal and decides on a second cup before trudging back upstairs to ready himself for another day at the agency.

In the mirror he notices the heavy black circles around his eyes, witnesses to his sleepless nights. Searching through the medicine cabinet for eye drops, he notes the absence of condoms. Reminding himself to buy some on the way home, he examines his body for sores and lesions.

Wait a minute ... Condoms? How could I ever have sex with Cal again? How could I even think of it? God! Sex?

"Buster?" He shouts from the bedroom. His voice echoes through the house, but Buster doesn't answer.

"Buster, honey?"

No reply.

Brad goes up to the third floor and slides a porn video into the VCR. Within seconds, he is hard. He beats off until a few drops of white land on his belly, a rather unspectacular display.

I've made the decision to make the most of my illness. I'll go through it quietly. I'll be too proud and dignified to let anyone see me struggling. I will save the ugliness for private places. When I start to lose weight, I won't accept visitors. I'll shut everyone out. Except Cal. It won't take much for people to figure out. I won't need to tell anyone a thing. Everybody will already know. Vicious, chattering queens. But I'll be better than that. I'll leave before the worst comes. I'll trick the disease. I'll kill myself before it kills me. I'll beat it. I'll win.

$$\Diamond \quad \Diamond \quad \Diamond$$

"Nardo?"

"Yes," says the receiver against Brad's face.

"It's Brad Chalmers."

"Hello, Brad. Are you feeling any better today?"

"Oh, not really. I have a migraine, but that's not why I called."

Silence. "Well, what is it, then?"

"I'd like you to give me a prescription."

"For what? What's the matter?"

"Well, that's up to you. I'd like you to prescribe something very strong so that when the time comes and I can't go on any longer, I'll have the pills to take ..."

"Perhaps we should make an appointment so you can talk about this in person."

"Don't change the subject."

"Brad, I've told you this before. I think you need coun-selling. It's not something I'm confortable discussing, and it's not something I do for my patients. Besides, you don't need any more bandaids for the way you feel. I'd like you to get into regular counselling, not pills, not homeo-pathy, not massage therapy or scented candle-dipping."

"Cut the crap, Nardo. You know what I'm saying."

"Yes, I do, Brad. You want a lethal dose of pills to cure an illness you don't even have. How dare you ask me such a question! How dare you insult all the people who are coping with this illness!"

"Whose life is it anyway?" Brad shouts and then slams the receiver into its cradle.

"Fucking asshole!" Brad rummages through a desk drawer and finds a small plastic bag bulging with an assort-ment of pills. He places two Valium on his tongue and washes them down with a sip of coffee. He replaces the bag in the drawer and brushes the bangs out of his eyes.

His assistant enters with a thermos in his hand.

"Would you like more coffee, Mr. Chalmers?"

Brad looks the other way, feeling the throbbing in his temples. He looks back at the telephone and grinds his teeth. "Oh, I could just stab!" he shrieks.

The young man puts the thermos at the edge of the desk and lowers his eyes.

"Get out," Brad says to him. "Get out. Get out of my office!"

He hurries through the first two hours distracted and sleepy from the Valium. A call comes through at 11:30. It's Cal. He wants to meet for lunch. Brad joins him an hour later, at Abbey's, a bistro run by a friend of theirs. The waiter, Peter, gives them a warm smile.

"We may be able to bid for the Thornton exhibit if they decide to take it on tour," Cal says. "I'm just afraid that the museum will make a higher bid. Anyway, I know the gallery would be a much better venue for it. Hopefully the Thornton organizers will realize that, too." Brad sips his wine and rearranges the cutlery, avoiding Cal's eyes.

"Is something wrong?" Cal asks.

"Bill Reid has run off and done another soft-porn video and still wants to do catalogue work for us," Brad drones. "Our most popular model does cheesy pornos and then bitches that clients won't hire him to pose in underwear."

"Do you realize that next week is our anniversary?" Call asks.

At first Brad can't believe what he's just heard. Then he remembers that he hasn't told Cal that he's ill. He has no idea. Brad nods with a bleak smile.

The anniversary looms before him, with all the ramifications pounding in his head. It's like being aware of silent screaming; he can hear it, but it doesn't make any sound at all — like a secret, Brad's secret. And Nardo's. Brad looks at Cal, seething.

"What's wrong?"

You infected me.

"Brad?"

Murderer!

"Brad!"

Who else have you infected?! Fucked?

"Here we go," Peter chimes out, arriving with their food. He sets the plates down gently and asks if they'd care for fresh pepper. As he turns to go fetch the phallic pepper mill, Brad's eyes are drawn to Peter's neck, just below the left ear, where he sees a small purple blotch – smaller than a dime. Brad freezes in his seat as Peter grinds pepper onto his salad. Brad's shoulders unlock as the waiter walks away, but he's still tied up in knots inside.

"Five years of living together," Cal says, lifting his glass.

Brad is squirming inside. Does it show? Can Cal see?

Cal gives Brad a warm smile. "Don't you think we should do something to celebrate? Like sneak away for a few days? New York, maybe? Or buy a new house? Abe says it's not a bad time to buy property right now. The market's pretty good."

"I don't know." Brad stabs at his salad.

"About what?" Cal asks. "Taking a trip or buying a house?"

"I don't know."

Cal sets down his cutlery with a clatter, pulling Brad from his trance. Cal looks at him, confused, but perhaps more disappointed, maybe even suspicious.

"Is there something wrong, Brad?"

Brad shrugs as if he doesn't understand, or doesn't really care to make the effort to understand.

"I don't know. You've been acting funny. Is every-thing alright at the agency? You took some Valium, didn't you? I can always tell when you're on Valium."

"The agency is exactly how it always is," Brad tells him, trying to sound animated. "My assistant is an incompetent bitch. And as for my, uh, drug intake, you just worry about what you put in your own mouth."

"What the hell do you mean by that?" Cal says in a controlled voice, his nostrils flaring.

And then it comes to Brad again, the creeping, crawling sensation that makes him want to wrap his hands around Cal's throat.

You infected me, you bastard! You killed me! And you've probably killed Buster, too!

He wants to scream it until he's hoarse, but the words aren't there, just anger, pure, raw. Brad downs his wine and motions to Peter for another glass.

Cal resumes eating, watching Brad. Brad focuses on his wineglass and tries to push the anger away, drown it. The waiter interrupts the busy silence to ask how they're enjoying their meals. Brad nods without speaking, taunted by the purple spot. Cal manages a few glowing adjectives, and Peter, satisfied, walks to another table.

Get those pills. Beat the clock. Kill it. Stab it. Let it bleed. Get those pills. Beat the clock.

When his third glass of wine arrives, Brad draws it immediately to his lips. Cal puts his cutlery down abruptly and glares. Brad notices a slight quiver in Cal's upper lip.

He's upset. I've provoked him. Good.

"Brad?" Cal shifts in his chair. "Tell me what the problem is. Whatever it is, I can handle it, okay?" He holds his gaze on Brad, who tries looking away, up, down. He sips his wine, doesn't respond.

Cal's voice changes. "Do you think you're being discreet? Clever?" There is a pause. "Well you're not. I know you too well, so let it go and tell me what's bothering you."

Suddenly Brad finds another voice speaking through him, cold and panicked. "Drop it. Alright?" He smiles. "Or would you care to have a scene right here?" The alcohol has snuck up on him and taken control of his perceptions, restraint, and everything else in his mind and body. It's as though he left the room fifteen minutes ago.

Brad can see Peter looking over from behind the cappuccino machine, his curiosity piqued by the outburst. Brad motions for the bill.

"What are you doing?" Cal asks. "I'm not finished yet."

Peter places the slip of paper on the table.

"I am," Brad says, throwing two twenties on the table and walking away. He hears Cal calling his name as he weaves to the front door.

A cool summer breeze revives him as he approaches his car. He drives, affected by the liquid lunch, to the office, where he informs his assistant that he must tend to a family emergency and won't be back for the rest of the day.

Within half an hour Brad is lying in a six-by-six cubicle, towel wrapped around his waist, available to anyone who passes by. He has sex three times before he leaves: no passion, no hugging or kissing, just flesh against flesh with no emotions involved. Except anger. He's never been good at venting his anger the right way.

Crash and burn, crash and burn. Live and let die. Never live, never learn.

Brad repeats the little poem to himself as he leaves, hurrying away from the bathhouse entrance, afraid of being seen and even more frightened by the possibility of remembering what he's just done. Fleetingly, he realizes that he goes to that bathhouse sometimes twice a week. It's not that he doesn't want to remember. He usually can't.

Oh God, I go to the tubs. Look at me! I've become a closeted, married man from the suburbs.

He goes down on them, straight or gay. Never thinks about it, never looks at their fingers for rings, or at their faces for worry lines about the eyes or at the corners of their mouths. The baths aren't about who you are or where you come from or anything else on the outside. Just cocks and holes and no questions asked. Just do it. And hurry up.

When he arrives home, Cal is frantic. "What the fuck is going on with you?"

"Leave me alone, you bitch."

God, can he smell the cum on me?

"That's great, Brad. You get drunk at lunch and don't speak to me, and then walk out without saying where you're going, and you're mad at me?! You are too much sometimes!"

"Yeah? Well enjoy it while it lasts."

Cal's mood softens. He moves toward Brad slowly, but Brad is afraid he'll get too close. He doesn't want to be touched. Somehow, Cal must sense this, stopping to lean against the hall closet door a couple of feet away.

"What do you mean by that?" he asks, sounding afraid. Getting no response, Cal shifts his weight and struggles with the awkward silence. "Look, Brad, I'm sorry. I don't want to yell at you. You know I hate it when we fight. But you've got to treat me like your partner because that's what I am. You can't act this way and expect it not to affect me. Tell me what's going on."

The telephone rings. Brad moves to answer it, but Cal stands in his way. Brad pushes up against him. Cal resists. When he turns to go around him, Cal moves to block him, but then relents and steps away.

Brad picks up the phone on the fourth ring. Dr. Nardo's voice shocks him. He feels blood flushing his cheeks as he turns his back to Cal. Nardo says he received an urgent message from his service from Cal this afternoon. Brad reassures him that everything is alright. But Nardo wants to speak to Cal.

"No. I'm sorry, it's not a good time right now, okay?"

"But ..."

"It's not a good time," Brad says. "I'll get him to call you later." He hangs up.

"Who was that?"

"None of your business."

Cal turns to leave. Brad leans toward the hallway and talks at him as he walks away. "Look, I'm exhausted and hungover, alright? Let me take a shower and we'll go from there, okay, pumpkin?" He's all sugary sweet now. It's another stall tactic, of course — and Cal knows it, too — but he agrees.

"I'll be waiting for you."

Brad steps into the tub and draws the curtain behind him. He releases a deep sigh as the hot water falls against his tired body, filling the bathroom with steam. He pulls the shower head back a bit and sits down under the invigorating spray.

He hears the bathroom door open, and looks up to see Cal pulling away the shower curtain. He crouches and leans over toward Brad, who trembles slightly as he gets near. Cal puts his arms around him. The panic dissipates. A calm sets in. Cal pulls out of the embrace and runs his hand through Brad's wet hair.

"Nardo called."

Brad's stomach turns. He moves back, turns off the water, looks awkwardly at Cal.

"He told me about your visit yesterday. About your worries. And your stability. We're both concerned about you." Brad clenches his teeth, fighting, fighting. Cal looks into his eyes. "Jesus, Brad. I'm ... I don't know what to say when you get like this. But we've gone through this before. Okay? It's not the end of the world ..."

"But it's the end!" Brad wails. "It is. Don't you know what all these symptoms mean?" He doesn't know how long the two of them stand there half-holding and seeing each other flush with embarrassment and fear, Brad's slender, glistening body against Cal's soaked shirt.

"You can't keep putting us through this," Cal wraps a towel around Brad's shoulders. "You've got to go see somebody."

"What did Nardo say? Did he tell you I need a shrink?"

"All he said was that he'd like you to be in counselling. And maybe go back on antidepressants. I have to agree with him, Brad. 'Cause I can't live like this. And you can't carry on this way. Do you realize how many assistants you've fired in the last four months?" Brad doesn't move, holds his breath. "Six. Six in four months. That's more than one a month."

"They were terrible," Brad stammers.

"But six in a row? What are the odds? Nardo has been your friend and your doctor for more than ten years. I think you should listen to what he has to say. And don't think everybody's ganging up on you. You get it in your head that the world's against you, and it's just not true."

Cal moves back and removes his shirt, throws the wet garment into the bathtub.

Brad notices that his nipples are erect.

"Honey, can't you see that this is a problem?"

I'm sick.

"Huh? Brad? Don't you think something's wrong to make you act this way?"

Fuck...

"Wouldn't you rather live a less complicated life? I would."

Off...

"There are psychiatrists and therapists and groups and programs all geared toward helping people live normal lives."

"Oh, great! A program! Perfect! A fucking group! A new shrink, another doctor. Get with the program. Who the fuck do you think I am? Your son? Your property?" Brad is breathing rapidly.

Cal takes a step back and shifts his glance to the floor. "My lover," he says quietly. "You're my lover. Okay? Don't do this. Don't make me leave. I know it's how you deal with things, Brad. I've seen you do it so many times. Where have all your friends gone? Why doesn't your sister call anymore? I'm the only friend you've got left. Don't do it to me too. Don't make me leave. Because I will, if you push me. You understand me?"

Brad moves to the bedroom and lies down on the bed, eyes glazed with tears and anger.

Cal sits at the edge of the mattress. Brad reaches a hand out and places it on his back. Cal turns to Brad and pulls his legs up onto the sheets. He takes Brad's hand in his own and then rolls over to face him.

They hold each other like they haven't in months. And they make love tenderly, quietly, as if somebody is waiting outside the door, waiting to break it down and steal everything the moment they look the other way. It's a feeling with which Cal has become familiar. It's not that he minds, really — he doesn't have a choice.

Brad pulls away emotionally, while Cal unwraps a condom, and wonders if he's safe, if he should cry or scream. What would Cal do? Would he leave? And then, as if by magic, the anger and harsh words vanish. Cal's hips rock gently against Brad's spread legs. He closes his eyes for a moment. Brad shifts his weight slightly. Cal stretches forward and kisses him on the mouth. Brad can't control the smile on his face. Cal moans and pumps harder. Brad raises his right hand to his face and pulls a string of hair out of his eyes. "Oh yeah," Cal mumbles. "Yeah, pumpkin. I'm gonna come." Brad moves his hips down, sending a slight pain shooting inside. "Do it," Brad urges. "I love you, pumpkin," Cal says. "I love you too, pumpkin," Brad replies, unaware that the condom has just split open.

love and war

take a deep breath. Okay. He's approaching. He's very close. No, wait. He's hesitating. He's hovering. He's looking, no, now he's looking away. Now he's coming again. Oh, god. He's standing right beside me, smiling. I smile back, pull my stomach in.

He speaks in a deep voice, his breath tinged with cider. I've been watching him, but I wasn't going to make the first move. Am I too chicken, too above it all, too desperate? Yes. I love and hate the funky horny sex feeling that meeting someone stirs in me; its itchiness, like having a rough wool sweater inside my heart and psyche, an uncomfortable, building, muted itch that I can't get rid of and don't really know if I want to.

I see people around me riddled with so much pain and fear that it's like a fire raging within them. Some try to extinguish it with alcohol. Others with drugs. Still others try to put it out with sex, but eventually it rises again and again. What are we lacking? Why doesn't it work for some people? *It*? Love, I mean. *It*, the feeling of being satisfied, or happy, even.

When winter hits, it seems that despair strikes harder than any cold or flu. It's when I most need a warm body pressed up against me, the feel of arms around me, arms that want to be there. But I go home to cold, crisp sheets and my cat. Purring is nice, but not enough.

Mr. Man just asks my name and extends a firm, masculine hand. How formal. By the time our hands meet I am already in hyper hormone drive. How long has it been? Five seconds? Long enough to know I want it and need it. And I'm feeling it for him in particular.

He flashes a smile of crooked teeth and I can imagine kissing him and putting my tongue in his mouth, and I have to step back for a second because this is all too much, too sudden, too hot, and I like to think about things. Or at least I like to think I do.

We dispense with talk of jobs, lovers, diseases, likes, dislikes, favourite singers, favourite movies, and what we want from each other. We've walked past each other before, eyed one another across the bar, looked, kind of, but not really long or hard enough for it to have meant anything – until now. It was just a quick glance, a cruisette. It didn't mean anything – nothing in these places ever means much – but tonight it means sex.

The bar has become redundant. We've connected. Billie Ray Martin drones out "Your Loving Arms" as we leave. Once inside his car he doesn't grab me like I want him to or kiss me like I wish he would or look at me like I think he should. He pulls out his wallet and shows me his police badge. He doesn't talk about his job as we drive to his place, and I wonder how much danger he's seen, how much more he knows about things and life and sex and doing it than I do. I find myself counting each second of silence and then blurt out whirling, stream-of-consciousness sentences, which is what I do when I'm nervous.

My thoughts dart about. He looks at me and asks me to repeat what I've just said. "This is a really nice car," I say. He nods as he drives.

I sit on his bed as he does a quick tidy-up. He does not bother to talk or even take notice of me. I could just as well be his vibrator waiting in a drawer. He wanders into the bathroom. While he's gone, I scan the room for hidden video cameras, hunting knives, shotguns, chains, ice picks, chainsaws and books on human anatomy. Finding none, I fidget on the bed trying to find a not-too-passive, yet not-too-aggressive pose to strike when he returns. After a shower, he shuffles some more papers and puts away some clothes.

He finally joins me on the bed, draws himself to me, kisses me — a sucking, passionate kiss. Then we have sex. It's good sex. It's fine. It's alright. The more I think about it, the less I think of it. The moment we're finished he doesn't just roll over, he rolls away.

The next morning I prepare to leave him for a cold, drizzling rain. I've only had about an hour's sleep. Mr. Man smells of yesterday's Obsession as we don't kiss goodbye. He doesn't hug me or shake my hand or tweak my nipple, or anything. As I walk out the door, I turn back to him and call, "Thanks."

At home I crawl into bed and try to fall asleep, but all I can think about is disappointment and a flicker of anger. Anger? Fuck, yes! The moment I acknowledge it, it explodes. His turning away the night before is burned on my brain. It was more forceful than any slap to my face, more alienating than any rejection, and far more emotionally draining than any insult.

So he turned his back to me. So? What did I want? What was I expecting? A ring and a U-Haul? Hardly. I had few expectations, if any. But I didn't expect such a nothing from having him near, his kisses still wet on me. I wanted to kick him and ask, "What do you think you're doing, mister man?! Huh?" But then I started shaking. Not from nerves, but from wanting to be held. And when I thought I would explode, the opposite happened; an eerie calm came over me.

I look down at my cat lying beside me in bed. He purrs and looks up, basking in my presence.

I don't think I'll hear from him. I absolutely do not expect him to phone me. I figure he's forgotten about the evening, maybe I'm even hoping he has. But I certainly won't forget it. I'm glad I feel disappointed and angry. I'd be worried if I felt nothing after trying to satisfy an urge and a need. Sex is an everyday thing. It's also Oz and Xanadu and home and comfort and fear and joy. It's two bodies coming together in motion and emotion. A-ha. Emotion. That's what was missing. Old fashioned? Hardly. I know what was lacking and now I know what I want. And if it's stupid and naive to want affection, then so be it.

I try to settle back into the silence of not having anyone I can talk to who understands my feelings. That makes me want it even more. *It,* again. I want *it.* I start making phone calls to friends in faraway cities and foreign countries. They'll understand, they'll know. And they do. My sister says that sometimes you have to keep learning the same lesson over and over again until it sinks in. Like an expensive moisturizer, it takes time to be absorbed into the skin and to erase those fine, visible lines.

I stop checking my answering machine ten times a day for messages. And so it comes as a surprise, almost a month later, when he calls. He apologizes for not having phoned sooner. He's been relocated to a different division and has been quite busy. And now he is talking to me and he wants me to come over. I think to myself, should I get fitted for a straightjacket before or after? But I go. And it's hotter, and nicer and better. When we're finished, he rolls onto his back and looks up at the ceiling. A minute later, he rolls back and wraps his arms around me. He curls into me, spooning like Al Pacino with the prostitute in *Frankie and Johnny*. He kisses the back of my ear and says, not whispers, "Thanks for coming over."

That was over two months ago. I dropped by his apartment last week. He wasn't there. The landlord told me that he'd moved closer to work. And that's the end of the story. *All is fair in love and war.* Sometimes I think they're the same thing.

positive i.d.

alex has a secret. Some baggage. And he wants — needs — to unload it. On me. I didn't ask him to tell me. But I listen.

Alex is HIV-positive. He expects me to leave the room or cry or walk away. All I can say is, "So?"

So? Not out of disrespect, or lack of compassion or lack of caring. So? Because it's so ordinary now. So common. So unremarkable. Is this how it feels to be alive?

Alex tells me how it happened. He was lonely. More lonely than any man should ever be. And he went out there to be touched, to feel something, he says. Is that all we really want to feel? That we're not alone? How long will it take? How many hands must touch us? This can't be right. What's wrong with us?

The attendant put him in room 100. Alex says this was the first sign that he shouldn't have come. The attendant said, "It's all I have left."

First floor at the baths. Only old hairy ethnic married men occupy rooms on this floor. You can see them there on the way in and out, and as you pass through the corridor on the way to the whirlpool. Alex scrawled his initials on the back of a chit, took the key and towel and waited to be buzzed in.

It was your basic bathhouse room. Alex opened the locker, hung up his clothes, wrapped the rough white towel around his waist, and ventured out. None of the doors to the other rooms on the first floor were open. Nobody was in the showers or saunas. The toilet stalls and whirlpool were vacant; perhaps everyone was sleeping.

Up on the second floor, all the doors but one were closed. He could hear the thumping of disco music from speakers situated throughout the hallways. No heavy breathing, no grunts or moans of encouragement drifted out of any of the rooms. If the first level is the harbour of the unshowered and desperate, the second floor is the fat floor. The second floor is only mildly more popular than the first. The third floor is the place to be.

When Alex got there he realized that he'd been had: It was ugly night. And skinny night. And ugly-skinny night. The third floor was a sham. He ascended the final flight to check out the fourth level.

Many men don't bother with the fourth floor; home of hookers, pushers, those seeking group encounters, guys who like to lick feet — feet that have trod the musty old carpets and God knows what else. What happens when they kiss someone afterward? Is there such a thing as Athlete's Mouth?

Alex peered into the locker room and, there, seated on the bench, was a normal-looking man. Alex says he was "pulling his pud." They exchanged looks. Alex gestured for the man to follow him. They descended the three flights of stairs and slipped into Alex's room where they removed their towels and began to massage each other.

Alex describes the encounter as fun, at first. But he was drunk. The five shots of tequila and four beers he'd downed at the bar beforehand had sufficiently anesthetized him for the excursion. One thing led to another. Alex said yes. For whatever reason. Or maybe no words were spoken at all.

"When I got home, I stripped down," Alex says. "I threw my clothes into a garbage bag, put the bag down the chute in the hall, and then took a long, hot bath. After I'd dried off, I stared at myself in the mirror, thinking I looked like somebody else. Somebody guilty. For twenty minutes I stood in front of the bathroom mirror, trying to figure out who it was I looked like. I smoked a cigarette and glared at my reflection in the mirror. Whore. Slut. Fuck-up. Zombie. I don't know why it happened," he says. He shakes his head from side to side. Lights a cigarette.

He's silent for a moment and I'm wondering where his common sense had gone, where his soul had gone, his passion, his love, his desire, his love of life – where had they all gone? Swallowed up. Devoured. Dissolved. And why?

"I don't know. It was a mistake."

And not an uncommon one. I've heard it many times before. Alex wasn't the first to be weak. He won't be the last. But I don't know why I can't feel sorry for him. Maybe it hits too close. Maybe I'm just an inch away from letting go. And I don't want to know what it means, don't want to know that I'm just as vulnerable. I am not better nor am I different from Alex – or anyone else. I am just as much at risk.

"So, does it bother you?" Alex asks.

"What? That you're HIV-positive?"

"Yeah."

"No. It doesn't," I lie.

bitter/sweet

i look over the pastel-grey sheet pulled up to my neck and there he lies; all youth and beauty.

My passion begins to stir again as I remember his hands gripping my shoulders, the rush of his breath in my face. I should say goodbye now, but I hesitate. His sleep allows me to.

Noticing the small brown mole on his neck, I remember kissing it somewhere between last night and this morning. His breast rises and falls with such delicacy that I fear my own breathing will wake him. His lips form a boyish pout. I kiss them with my eyes, taking all of him in, studying his profile as if for a test.

I take in his room. There are pictures of James Dean and Montgomery Clift on the walls. By the mirror is Marilyn Monroe captured in black and white, caught between genius and torment, love and fear. I breathe it into my lungs.

The light changes. The sun is coming up. Or maybe it's just me adjusting to my surroundings, becoming wary. But of what? Not him — he's just a young man, a boy, really. I am conscious of our differences.

He wanted to know everything about me; where I was born, what I do for a living, what music I like, the types of movies I see. We talked about coming out to our parents and the silences we endured afterward.

I don't go home with many people and he believed me, I think, when I told him. Of course it's true – why lie to a stranger? But then, why not lie?

He spoke of his previous relationship and his inability to meet trustworthy men since it ended. I made no attempt to convince him I was Prince Charming making a dashing rescue from a life of loneliness, although that's exactly what I want to do.

Instead it was he who comforted me – with his body, his honesty and his passionate, gentle sex.

I rise from the bed and, slowly gathering my clothing from the floor, dress quietly and turn to the window. I look out across the river at the cool city rising and shining in the bursting streaks of sun that overpaint its stark shades of black and grey.

As my eyes turn, they are caught by a picture on the wall. It's a photograph of my companion smiling, wrapped in the arms someone his age.

"He's dead," comes a voice heavy with ... is it sleep?

A dark mop of hair covers his eyes. He pulls it back and sits looking at me as if waiting for a response. I shrug, not knowing what to say.

How I long to kiss his plump lips and place my hands on his shoulders, but the kind thoughts and comforting gestures stay nestled in my head.

"Shall I make some coffee?"

I shake my head and move to collect my socks. He stares at me.

"Is something wrong?"

"No," I say. "It's nothing to do with you. You are lovely."

"Derryck ..." He doesn't say anything more. I fumble with the silence.

"When did your friend die?" I surprise myself by asking. I want to run away and make a clean break, ashamed of my intrusion.

"About two years ago. We had been lovers since our second year at university."

I'm so sorry. "This is the relationship you were telling me about last night?"

He nods, avoiding my glance.

"How did he die?"

"Pneumonia."

I find myself sitting beside him on the bed. He reaches over and does up the top button of my shirt.

"I haven't been tested yet. I don't know whether it's because I'm afraid or ... whether it's just the wrong time to put myself through the stress."

"It's a difficult decision, but I think it's worth knowing."

"Have you been tested?"

I nod and chuckle quietly, re-experiencing the relief. I flash through the half-dozen eulogies I've delivered in the past few years; the words, the tears, the speechless moments staring into the eyes of partners, friends, and parents and the empty hours in the days and weeks after the last of my friends had died, knowing that the phone wouldn't ring anymore. And that I had no one to lunch with. Sometimes I wonder why I'm the only one left, why my once-shining circle of friends has become a solitary point of dim light. I have no answers. I have no more tears. I am dry. A survivor, they say.

"It's difficult making new friends," I say. "I don't ..." I stop myself, set my limits. I cannot break down. He ignores the silence, puts his hand in mine. I look once again at the picture of the two laughing men.

"Can I see you again? Will you leave me your number?"

I bend over quickly to tie my shoelaces to hide the rush of anxiety. Run, run!

"What do you want with somebody like me?" I stand up in front of him. "You should find somebody a little closer to your age and fall in love with him." What a stupid thing to say.

"Oh, thank you. Just like that?" He pauses and sends me a look that says I should know better. "Things don't work out that way."

I look into his eyes. "Maybe so, but things don't work out this way either." Brent. That's his name.

He reaches out and takes my arm, pulling me back down onto the bed. I feel his warm breath on my neck. He whispers, "How do you know?" quietly in my ear. He kisses me lightly, his mouth moving about mine. Then he pulls his head back and looks at me seriously. "Won't you stay for a little while? I've got the day free and I'd love to spend it with you. Please?"

I run my fingers through his hair, like a parent. I say no, that I'm sorry. Then I stand up. I walk a few steps toward the door and he calls for me to wait. I look back at him and he's scribbling something on a piece of paper at his nightstand.

He pushes the covers off and comes to me, extending the note. He is naked. I see the cyclone shape of his chest hair, fanned out between his nipples and narrowing as it descends to his navel. I drink his beauty in.

"Thank you, Brent, for making me feel so wanted. I had a wonderful night with you, but now I have to leave."

"I hope you'll call, Derryck." Avoiding his gaze, I step into the hallway and look up just as the door swings shut.

I stand in the hall for a moment. I count to ten, slowly. To twenty. And then thirty. Still I feel no sense of relief. I should have stayed. He wanted me to. But I have a life to go back to. He's too young for me. How I wish I could change everything. I wish I could let myself fall.

For a split second I consider knocking on the door and lying in his arms again. I feel the knot tightening in my stomach as I walk to the elevator.

The door slides open. My throat tightens and I swallow hard, looking back, checking to see if he's peeking out the door, but the hallway is dark. I undo the top button of my shirt and step into the elevator.

room for patrick

i hear his voice calling me and I follow it, rounding the corner toward the quiet room. I pause with my hand on the doorknob, waiting to hear him again, but there is only silence.

Once again I have been pulled from an uneasy sleep. Lately, the waking hours outweigh the precious sleep they interrupt. I walk through the empty house. Today it doesn't feel as if I own it, but rather that it owns me. It's not that I want to leave ... I only wish it made me feel different.

The door creaks open. My eyes dart about the room as if I expect him to be sitting there, at his computer table with glasses pushed down to the edge of his nose and fingers slowly striking the keys, making that familiar, comforting clicking sound.

I drifted through periods of emptiness, past houses and relationships, easy love, complicated sex, a life of doors that seemed to open so easily. It was child's play. I stumbled into faceless nobodies in the crowds, following them around city blocks and into secret places where, left alone with only our skin in common, we came quickly together, broke passionately apart. It was simple. My heart only fluttered momentarily before back to the drudgery of my life I would crawl, invigorated, satisfied, and perhaps a little surprised. The feeling wouldn't come yet. Not yet. There was much emptiness in the world to experience.

There was one writer before Patrick, several years before. A thin, punkish young man, David Thorn, who was angry and spoke for his generation. I wondered if he ever noticed me staring at him from across the way, or following a tidy seven steps behind him on the way to the baths, where I would stand behind walls and doors, watching and waiting. And when I learned my thin prince was ill, I reread all of his books, hoping to find something I could construe as my own, a character's flaw or quirk that nobody had picked up on and that I could coddle and cradle in my heart, as if to encourage it to become a part of me. But I found nothing I could steal.

When David died, I burned his books. The relationship was over. He was gone. And nobody else would speak of what had happened. The fact of my love, its proof, and his love for me, burned away, all cinders and smoke and nothing. I didn't say goodbye. I burned him.

Anyone can tell you it's easy to fall in love. But how easy is it to fall in love with someone who is removed from you, someone who thinks the extent of their relationship is to sign their name on a copy of their book, and perhaps smile when you tell them how moving their writing is, and how you feel as though you know them, feel close to them. And they smile, dot the *i* in their name, and then focus on the next person in line. At first I thought Patrick would be impenetrable, his fortress secure. At first.

Patrick wasn't eager to listen to me in the beginning. Perhaps he couldn't hear my nervous voice praising him, pushing him onto a pedestal. I suspect my voice was drowned out by the sound of the clock ticking in his ears, for he seemed to not really notice me. But yes, I persisted. And yes, I can read. I read all about it, how he wanted no new friends, as he had no energy left to give. Just enough for the people he already knew. Anything you wanted from him was on the page. That was how you had a relationship with him, by reading his words. And that was the extent of it. But not for me. I wormed my way in despite his protestations, as if his speaking voice did not have the weight or strength of his writing. I found my way to him. His words told me to come.

There is a picture of the two of us. It hangs, framed in brass, on the wall opposite me. In it, Patrick looks down at something on the ground, and I, beside him, darkened by shadow, stare at him reverently. I hardly recognize that expression now, although the picture is only a few years old, taken without our knowledge and before the tidal wave crashed down on us. I am in love. At least in the picture I am.

I fix my gaze on the mirror beside the photograph and

see the harsh, indifferent look on my careworn, weather-beaten face. Wrinkles are creeping in around my eyes. I look away, not knowing what to make of myself anymore.

I remember it was one afternoon as I sat watching him dozing lightly – he rarely slept deeply, if at all, in the last few weeks – that I knew I was exactly where I wanted to be: beside Patrick Mann. But I felt oddly displaced, as if I was observing my reality and not actually experiencing it, perhaps as though I had read it over and again in a book and had committed it to memory. But there I was, in Patrick's room, beside the IV drips and the vanity stocked with plastic bottles of various sizes and colours, thinking to myself, you're here, Billy. You're in Patrick's room. You're in Patrick Mann's fucking bedroom! And there he was, just a few feet away, so close, so very close. And he was on the shelves, on the walls, and in the picture frames and unopened letters in the hallway, and in the scraps of paper and shopping lists and parking tickets. He was everywhere.

For a moment I thought he sat up in bed and smiled at me as if he had just read my thoughts. And he said in a steady and clear voice that it was okay. Remember, he said. Remember.

I blinked and he was sound asleep on the bed. The nurse came in for her rounds. She was a slim, ghostly white woman with a stern, angular face. Around her I felt out of place. She may have been here longer than me, but I loved him. She changed his sheets, bathed and dried him, and looked after him. I fed him his baby-food meals and pills and held his hand and emptied myself to and for him. I was here because I wanted to be. Certainly not a major character, but I was there between the lines I had written.

◊   ◊   ◊

I let out a deep breath and walk into the room. I've avoided Patrick's study since the apex of his illness, keeping it in the back of my mind while he grew thinner and weaker. Between gasps he made me promise to sort everything out and send some snippets of poems to friends and family. I'll save the short stories for myself, going against the urgings of acquaintances in the publishing industry who want them for an anthology. An anthology of writings by dead writers. How gallant. How greedy. We disappear, we mourn, we purge, we profit. It's a new cycle, a new cycle of life. A life cycle.

But I will cling to Patrick's work selfishly, hold it in, keep it from a world that values a man's work more after his last breath escapes him, once his flesh and bones have been ravaged with sickness, his body cleansed in a sea of flames. Maybe one day I will change my mind. But, for now, I will carry the weight of Patrick's legacy, carry it like a doomed child. Whatever else remains, his private self, clings to me. It must, and I must have it. I will not allow anything else to change.

◊   ◊   ◊

I've poured myself a brandy and, snifter in hand, I sit at Patrick's wide oak desk and lift a page off of the disorganized pile. In his frail scrawl, Patrick lives on, as strong and as stable as his love for me. I pray my memory of him will last as long as his words on paper. Perhaps he won't change the world after all – I know he wanted to – but he changed mine. I believe that is enough.

Here I am, as inexperienced as I was when I first met Patrick, except now I feel as though I've had the wind knocked out of me, like something other than my hope is missing. I can't expect that I'll be able to get back on track or that I'll feel anything other than emptiness again. The most I can hope for is that one thing in this world will be permanent – my anger. It clogs my thoughts and pulls me out of bed in the mornings when I feel like hiding. I don't have room for laughter or envy or guilt or pride. I have to fight just to forget what I've lost in order to love. And what I've done to receive it. And where I must go and what I must do and which words need to be said and written down and remembered and which words need to be forgotten. Not Patrick's. Never.

There's a picture of Patrick on the wall. On the beach with a background of sand and a rising tide, he smiles, nostrils flaring, black hair, he glows, even in black and white. Inside the back flap of his last book is another picture I can't forget. His face is creased and expressionless, as if the camera had stolen his soul. His eyes are dead. Somebody's thick, muscled arm extends from behind him, hand resting on his shoulder — a hospital worker or doctor perhaps. These two images collide in my mind, make me want to leave the corridors and smells of bleach and urine and pain and collapsing fear. Want to go back to the beach. To feel the sand between my toes and the waves rushing at me, chasing and testing me. Can I stand still as the water crashes down at my feet, or will I spin and falter? I don't know. I don't know what my anger wants me to do because it's tired and can't bring Patrick back or bring me back. So what good are pictures? Maybe words are all we need.

Hoping to comfort me, friends say that saints and angels hover above us, to guide us. I don't believe it. I don't believe in anything anymore except ire and death. I feel them and see them every day. I know them. They have found a friend in me. The truth of life — all life — is suffering. And the secret of life is transcending what makes you suffer. Patrick's words taught me that. The saints and angels will have to sing long and loud before the ignorance drains from millions of ears and the voices can be heard. But, for now, the ignorant have no access to his words, they have no room for him in their hearts. So they remain in darkness. But to those of us who can hear them,

Patrick's words sing. That is my solace.

Tomorrow I will call the publisher and release what is left on his desk. It doesn't belong to me. It might make a difference to somebody else. I don't want it. Let the world have it. The parting words of a saint who delivered of himself to anyone who would listen. The words will float and drown and cool and boil and fester and simmer and burn. Little explosions after the bomb has been dismantled. Tiny bliss, tortured hiss, a sea of sand and minds damned. Words. Only words.

Perhaps when the anger becomes joy there will be room for Patrick in our hearts. Perhaps then they will be able to hear.

Footsteps. I turn around and find William descending the staircase with a baseball bat in his hand. I close my eyes for a second. His voice opens them.

"How did you get in here?"

"I live here. Who are you?" I know who he is. He is Patrick Mann's lover, William. But I don't think he should be here.

"You were told to stay away," he says, his voice rising. "Far away from this house. Do you know how much trouble you're in now? Billy?"

"This is my house."

"This is my house, you fuck! Move against the wall," he barks. "What were you doing in there?"

"In Patrick's room?"

"Yeah! I said move against the wall!" He waves the baseball bat above my head. I turn around and stand against the wall. "Don't move. I'm phoning the police."

"I wasn't trying to steal anything," I lie. "I just wanted to be here."

"You're violating the restraining order, you little shit!" He moves into the kitchen and picks up the phone.

"Yes, I've caught a trespasser in my home. My name is William Curtis. 126 Nichol. Can you send somebody right away? Yes. Yes. No, he hasn't. I don't think so. Yes, I will. Thank you."

I sit down on the floor, my back to the wall. I want to leave now.

"Don't you fucking move," William says. "I'll kill you with my bare hands."

"Okay, okay," I say quietly. "I'm not going to hurt you. I just wanted to be inside."

◊   ◊   ◊

William looks at me. His anger melts slowly. He puts the baseball bat down and sits down beside me, embraces me, cries into my shoulder.

"You don't know what it's been like, Billy," he sobs. "Trying to have a private life with people who thought Patrick belonged to them. I got my first good night's sleep three days after he died. I was so relieved."

"Okay, William, it's okay." I rub his back as he cries into me. I see the baseball bat lying behind him.

"I can't understand why people want to devour their heroes. Anything that people wanted, it's all in his work. It's not anywhere else. Everything you and the rest of the world needs is in his writing. The rest of him, when he was alive, was for his friends and his family. Don't you see?" He pulls back from me.

I wipe some tears away from his face and put my hand on his shoulder. He continues sobbing. I move to stand up. William doesn't try to stop me. He just keeps sobbing — over what he's lost, I guess.

"Do you want a cup of tea?"

"Sure," he says. "If you don't mind."

"Not at all. You rest there. I'll put the kettle on."

I move around William and stoop down to pick up the baseball bat. I raise it in the air and swing it down hard on his head. There is a loud crack. A trickle of blood runs down his face. He collapses forward.

"Mine." I say to William's body. I drop the bat to the floor and close my eyes, thinking I hear a voice. But whose?

I open my eyes and see William at the front door. Two policemen enter. One removes a set of handcuffs. The other pulls his gun out of the holster, ready.

bad emotional risk

"I've always told you that you weren't built for dating," my friend Ronald says over an expensive cup of coffee.

"Oh, so you think it's my fault that I only date ridiculous men?"

"It's all in your perceptions, Brian. There's something wrong with you. I just haven't been able to put my finger on what it is."

"You've put more than your finger on what usually gets me in trouble." I smile.

"Yes, and never again, as the saying goes."

Ronald is an ex. An ex-whatever. We had sex a couple of times, went out for dinner, and then realized that we'd taken things about as far as they could go. As soon as the pressure to be on our best behaviour was gone, we developed a frighteningly honest friendship.

"Who said I was offering?"

"You know, for somebody so critical of other people, you are remarkably blind to your own faults."

"Yes," I say. "I'm a human being. Gloriously flawed. Take it or leave it."

"I have and I did," Ronald quips, smiling into his coffee cup.

"Do you want to hear about this guy, or what?"

"If it'll make you feel better, go ahead."

"Last Monday night I was working at the restaurant, and this guy and an older woman come in and sit on the patio. He's tall and a bit skinny, but boyishly cute, you know? We exchange glances and somehow I get involved in their conversation. As they're getting ready to leave, he goes downstairs to the bathroom. She pays the bill and asks for my phone number for him.

"I tell her that I usually don't give out my phone number, especially when the person isn't brave enough to ask for it himself. She's embarrassed and says she's just trying to help. She says that he's shy. So I write my number down on a slip of paper and give it to her. He resurfaces and they leave.

"When I get home that night there's a message on my machine from him. His name is Jeff."

"Did he have a big dick?" Ronald interrupts. "That's what this whole thing is about, isn't it?"

"No, it's not another big dick story. Be patient, would you?"

"So what happened?"

"We arranged to go on a date."

"Uh-oh. He had it coming, then."

"Shut up! So we go on this dinner date. He's cocky, you know? He's condescending to the waiter, which does not impress me, and there's this almost combative tone to his conversation all through dinner. Like he's got something to prove. It's kind of amusing for a while, but there's an edge to it that gets really annoying. Anyway, I drink too much wine, of course, which literally translates into take me, I'm yours. So we go back to his place. He owns this nice condo down by the lake and he puts on some soft music and it's all very romantic. But when I start to look around, I notice all these Barbie dolls everywhere. And then he starts to show them to me. He tells me he's a collector. Oh my god, of all people, I've gone home with a man with a Barbie fetish! I think I laughed at the collection, which wasn't very nice, I know, but just imagine a condo filled with Barbies and this cute, masculine guy. Oh yeah, and he smokes."

"Eeeww."

"I know. So we're in bed and, you know, we're having sex, and all of a sudden he stops and says that he'd really like to fuck me. I just look at him and say, 'Yeah? Well I'd like to fuck you.' I'm just mocking him when I say it, you know? And he just kind of smiles and tells me again that he wants to fuck me.

"I said, 'I heard you the first time.' And he says, 'I've got condoms and lube and your ass is so hot.'"

"Porno talk," Ron interjects.

"Yeah, you know, which is fine on a porn video, but not from a real live human being. Anyway, I say to him, 'Why don't I fuck you first and then you can fuck me?' And he says, no, he only gets fucked when he's in an intimate relationship."

"Are you serious?"

"Yes! Only when I'm in an intimate relationship. An intimate relationship! And this is where I lost it. So I go, 'Oh! It's alright for you to fuck me and we've just met, but I can't fuck you?' And he says, 'Yeah.' I can't believe my ears. I ask him if he realizes how stupid that is and how hypocritical and he says that he doesn't think so. He says that anal sex is something very intimate and is appropriate only within a trusting relationship. And I say, 'Yeah, but it's alright for you to go ahead and fuck me? You wouldn't actually be involved in the proceedings? It would be kind of like me sticking a dildo up my ass, right?' Except he's the dildo. Like I'm the whore and he's totally innocent and not involved. This makes no sense at all. And then do you know what he says to me?"

"What?"

"He says, 'I should have known from the fact that you're a waiter that you were a bad emotional risk.' "

"What?" Ronald can hardly contain himself.

"A bad emotional risk. Because I'm a waiter. I mean, my god! He's an insurance salesman who collects dolls. And he doesn't think he's really there when he fucks someone. What does that make him, a good catch?"

"Where do you find these men?"

"I have special skills. I'm a bad emotional risk."

"So then what, did you leave?"

"No. We finished having sex."

"Because he had a big dick?"

"Of course. Then I left."

"You're so distant and cruel."

"I'm a bad emotional risk, what do you expect?"

"Have you heard from him since?"

"Yeah, he kept calling, asking to go out again."

"Did you?"

"No. I haven't returned his calls. Think he'll get the

message?"

"Why not tell him the truth?"

"People don't want to hear the truth, Ronald."

"They don't?"

"No."

"Is that why you don't want to see this guy again, 'cause he called you a bad emotional risk?"

"Maybe. Or maybe it's because he said that and still wanted to go out with me."

everything

i am riding in on a kiss. A kiss that whispers across miles, down streets, through walls and curtains and heavy wooden doors. A kiss that seeps in between thin layers of skin as we brush and bristle against one another, remembering, forgetting, hesitating, building momentum, then stopping abruptly.

"No. Wait. Together this time." That's what you said. I remember the sensation of saliva between our lips, of dewdrops on chest hairs reflecting off tight, darkened nipples. A small pool in the hollow of a belly button. A careless wash of liquid – yours, mine, ours. This kiss reminds me, binds me to you.

Your ring is on my finger. It's a little too tight, and maybe you wanted it that way. I don't mind the hurt. The ring serves me well, is a part of me all the time even though you can't be. Sometimes I'll look down in the middle of an afternoon and see it there on my hand. And I'll want to get to you, but I must wait. Wait until Friday evening to board the plane. It's always me that comes to you.

At my desk, I drift from the words and numbers into the calm and steady arms that guide us to the bedroom, into the darkness of what we do. I kneel, waiting for you to put the chain around my neck so I can belong to you.

I breathe you in. But I am suffocating here, cut off by telephones and computer screens and bitter coffee. But today, Thursday, is different. I shake and hunger and cannot — will not — wait another day. I leave my life and come to you empty and needing.

The knowledge of you is the only complete thing I own. Apart from this ring and the collar I wear in your company and my frequent-flyer points, I have no valued possessions. I have few needs outside the black we create together, of feeling you hovering above me in the darkness. Nothing else. That's all I want.

There is a man seated beside me on the plane. He has a delicate face and strong hands. And while he sleeps beside me, I think about his body and wonder what he looks like naked in a cold room. I could pull him into me, offer him a warm place and two desperate arms to hold him as he dives into me, but it's not the same. I look down at his crotch, feel nothing.

How would you feel if I took you over, if I held you down and went at you, staring you in the eye and pressing you down on a couch or a chair or the floor and forced you to remain silent while I whispered orders, questioned your stability, stole your control, demanded your surrender? If I were bigger than you. If you wanted me to. If I wanted to. Or needed to.

I shuffle through the sliding doors at the terminal with a rehearsed sheepishness, hoping you'll see my hunger. But how would you know I'm here? I'm a day early. I pull at your ring. It stretches the skin at the base of my finger. It feels like I'm being cut. And it feels. Good.

I pull my suitcase through corridors, lurch into the backseat of a cab and wonder how big the driver's cock is, if he wants me to touch or suck it or come on his balding head or in a less public place, dollops of thick white discarded carelessly. I glance into the rearview mirror and notice his eyes on me, steel eyes. "What?" And he grins an aging man's smile with thick lips that seem to need kissing and I fall backwards, wondering why I come all this way through all these men and untouched bodies, through sleepless nights and cigarettes, through overflowing lives, distorted emotions, the memory and the smell of you and us, and you over me, rocking me, your hard cock, your rough hands, taking me away, there, right now, taking me there right now.

I have a copper key to let myself in, just in case. I've only had to use it twice. Usually you're at the airport to meet me, in your suit, with your briefcase. Sometimes a wink. Often a smile. Always a promise. How out of character it is for me to surprise you like this.

I anticipate the smell of your house; a combination of new carpet and incense. It's as much a part of you as the eyelids I will trace with my tongue. I will bury my face in the warmth of your armpit. You'll jerk when I do this; it's made you shoot even when I wasn't touching your cock.

Oh fuck. I'm so close. Stop.

I close the door behind me, silently calling your name as I turn the latch. This sound is a comfort. I move down the hallway, leaving my suitcase by the door, in case you're angry. I know I shouldn't have come. I didn't ask you. You're not expecting me. And I have no idea what I might find when I climb the stairs and, like a child, timidly open your bedroom door. Forgive me. I'm sorry. Yes. I'll do that.

There's a rushing sound about me, cars passing outside or blood coursing though my veins, the feeling of you is always with me. The blindfold against my eyes, my fingers on your flesh, the smell of your breath, the taste of your spit, the size of you invading me, reclaiming me. The sound of the feeling of you reverberates in my head and hands, in my ass. Thank you. Thank you for stepping in. Thank you for fucking me.

I lie down on the bed, close my eyes, and wait. I wait for a car engine, or a telephone, or a penis hardening and pressing up against white cotton, stretching, engorging, blood pumping. I wait to be pulled into the darkness. I wait for the sound of sweat as it beads on your chest, back and forehead and rolls down in tiny rivulets, down your tight body, down to the gap of your thigh where it clings to your hairless skin and then presses up against me.

I wake up. It is dark. You've got your mouth around the head of my cock. Your hands grip the base tightly. I hear it. I feel it. You let go of me with one hand and reach toward my face. I don't know what you're about to do. I'm three-hundred-billion nerve endings twitching, shivering, waiting.

My hands reach up to look for you, your thick cock, angry and hard. I grab it and pull you over, pull your cock into my mouth. You let go of mine and breathe loudly. I let the saliva rush and flow and spill out of my lips and down the skin of your dick. It spreads around and down my chin. I feel your balls, firm and round, and you moan and I want more, all of you.

You move away. I hear a child wailing in the back of my mind, so hungry and needy. There is a bounce on the mattress. You place a cool, moist object in my hand. I find your cock, slide the object over the tip, and unravel it. I can feel myself becoming lighter and I moan and mmmm and yes and then you're inside.

Your hands pull me up, turn me around so that, if I could see, I would be staring you in the face with you fucking me on your lap. I feel the muscles contracting in your legs and thighs. In my mind's eye I see your long hard cock sticking up inside me. You thrust. My insides flush with pain. A finger finds my mouth. Then two. I suck, sliding my tongue in and around them. The taste of skin and man. Your cock is strength and anger and control, the things I want you to make me feel because they don't come from me.

"Fuck. Oh, I'm so fucking close."

Your body shifts backward, your cock slides out. My hands rush forward as you fall back onto the mattress. You tear the blindfold off. I grasp your hard cock, re-move the condom, and pull the engorged flesh up and down, the need to feel you inside me stronger than ever. Shifting my weight, I go down on your right armpit, my tongue swirling around the patch of hair that tastes of sweat and skin and sex. Your body jerks. You're coming. The sound of your voice is primal. I feel the warmth on your chest as I rub your come-covered skin. Then I brace my own swollen cock and, with your semen as my lubricant, stroke up and down with silent ferocity, wishing you were always inside me.

This is everything, this is all. And I don't care if I have to leave my life to get here, to this place, with this feeling and you inside and on top. And I don't care. I cup my hands around this feeling and hold fast.

ask no questions

It's been a year since mother died and sometimes I feel her presence more now than when she was alive. When parents are gone physically, it seems as though their spirit has been strengthened, if only because we think we will be released. But there is no escape, no running from the past. And because I realize this, I am safe visiting my parents' house, with what is left of my father gliding through its rooms like a shadow, and a withering menagerie of pets and plants; testaments to mother's need for dependents.

I am a grownup with a business, with a life of my own, so what's this funny feeling, these memories that bleed from the walls? I'm not unhappy spending time looking out my old bedroom window at the sun reflecting on sheets of ice that cling to the skeletons of trees. I am not unhappy at all. But I long to feel a fire burning inside, or, rather, I long for the feeling of longing.

If actions do speak louder than words, what do you do when you can't feel the actions, can't feel anything?

Dad, do you want me to get some more wood for the fire?

Downstairs, the fireplace is lit. Father has spent the last twenty minutes easing himself up and down the creaky cellar stairs to retrieve chips and splinters. And I see how he sits before the fire, newspaper spread in front of his face as he strains through his glasses to pick out words. Sometimes sentences confuse him or slip from his memory's grasp. I used to envy his ability to articulate even the most complex thoughts. Now I wonder what he thinks, what he means when his sentences come out jumbled, aborted. I wonder when – and how – logic escapes us.

Father is in the La-Z-Boy, adjacent to the large chesterfield that pre-dates my arrival in the family. Its cream silk brocade is beautifully preserved; a relic, an object to be admired but never used. Like a human heart.

Something is missing at my father's feet. Rollie. That is why I am here. Rollie was put down yesterday and I am here to express my condolences. Named after mother's second stillborn child, Rollie was assigned the role of the perfect infant. If she were here now, momma would have put a pot of coffee on, wiped her hands on her skirt and said, "Well now, that's finished business." If momma were here now, I wouldn't be.

Dad, do you want me to give the extra dog food to the neighbours?

I can almost say that momma was most alive when those around her were suffering, usually at her hand. Mother's concept of love was along the lines of, what makes you suffer loves you. Mother must have loved us very much.

It's okay now. I've worked it through, as friends, doctors, and books have instructed me to. But still, I cannot help but feel sorry for her. For being so far away, for not believing in passion, for stifling her dreams, and expecting the world to accompany her in silent agony. I admired her because she understood control, although it served no one but her. I hate her because she left me. But what good is the hatred now? It's a dirty antique that cannot be cleaned. And so it stands there, tarnished, weary, perhaps trying not to attract too much attention. Hatred is a lamp that doesn't light.

Dad, don't you ever get lonely?

He's fallen asleep, pages of the newspaper fanned out across his lap. His head is tilted back, mouth open. His cheeks have shrunk. He has grown old.

I scribble a note saying I'll be back in time for dinner. It's a family tradition to leave notes. It seems the less we say to each other, the better we communicate.

Dad, are you disappointed in me?

It's not his responsibility, really, to make me feel better. He'd only be surprised by the question, and then lie. Of course, he'd say. I'm proud my only son is homosexual. Glad to know you won't have to know the routine of fatherhood and marriage. I'm pleased you've made a life for yourself out of an illness. Thrilled to know you take it up the ass. You have your hands full with your business and your ... friends. A relationship would only drag you down. Besides, who wants to see the person they love getting older and dying? Enjoy your life, son. Be the best you can be. Have some fun and find something interesting to write on your tombstone. Isn't that what your life is all about?

But I would never ask that question. It's too late to change things. Besides, I'm sure I'll need something to feel guilty about when I'm older; the mistakes I've made, the money I've lost, the people I've hurt, love I never felt reciprocated. Guilty about hating people who say they love me. Guilty about men.

Men like Don who didn't love me and Mike who couldn't and Frank who wouldn't and Rick who loved everyone else. What have I learned from them? Everything, because I've learned so much about what not to do. Nothing because I'm disconnected from that knowledge now. It sits there, sleeping. Like father.

Don was just a boy, as I was. He was the first inaccessible man I loved physically and emotionally. He was the painting I could never afford to buy, but looked at anyway. He might have loved me. For a while I believe he did. As a friend.

I fell for Mike, but he didn't, couldn't, wouldn't catch me. His love was a stress-free life filled with lust and lies and drugs and alcohol and a stubborn refusal to let go. I could not love him enough. Nobody could. I still chase him today, in my mind. He is buried in his parents' plot in a London, Ontario, cemetery. Loving son, brother and uncle.

Frank was married and loved sex. We had fun, conversation, compassion. We understood and accepted each other, but he could never love me, could never leave his wife.

Rick still dances in the recesses of my memory. I fixate on his boyish looks, the feel of his face in my hands, the softness of his lips, the way his eyes looked down at the ground when he talked to me and the sound of his words when he lied. Now he lives three thousand miles away in a warm place with books and movies and men to distract him.

Dad, how do you know when you've found the one? How do you know when to give up?

How I wish I could ask him. Tell him. So many things he's wanted not to know about. So much stands between us: the confusion, fear, ignorance about how our hearts work, why we do the things we do, and my homosexuality. The generation gap can't account for it all. What separates us, attracts us to this strange discomfort? I am not the man my parents hoped I'd be. Who is responsible? If anything was ever expected of me, I somehow managed to disappoint them. Should I feel guilty? Inadequate? A failure? Well, certainly not a success.

Hey, dad, what did you want to be when you were a boy?

My collection of photographs is a jumble without chronology; faces and places from yesterday, elsewhere, out of reach. Like so many things, it seems that the people in the pictures were meant only to appear, be photographed, and then leave before the images were developed. I keep them because I'm afraid that, otherwise, I will forget to feel anything at all.

Here's one of me and my cat Fluffy. She's just a blur in the picture, as she jumps out of my arms. One of the family, starched and sitting up straight. One of me in university when I dyed my hair black. My sister at age five or six, looking impatient. What was she waiting for? And me as a boy in black and white, at a birthday party, about to cry. Who comforted me, and who continued snapping pictures?

What if so much has been taken away that we have nothing else to possess except the things we've lost? Who can sit us down with assurances that everything is going to be alright? No lover, friend, career, sum of money, possession can provide what we do not have. I have not found it in books or learned it from therapists or heard it in pop songs, or gleaned it from the life experiences of others. It is something that just goes on, this vacancy. This desire to keep sleeping, deep sleeping, and the yearning to wake up with one little reason to not lay back down again.

Dad? What if everything isn't going to be alright?

for the love of ella

It's three o'clock on a Thursday afternoon and we've got the pre-weekend jitters, those jolts of anxiety when we can't wait for the excess of Friday night so we can sleep in on Saturday morning and avoid our hangovers. Marcy likes to do tequila shooters. We line them up and compete to see who can drink the most without heaving. Marcy is very competitive. If she were a man, she'd probably run around bragging about the size of her dick. But based on her proportions as a woman, I'm sure nobody would be impressed. That's not to say that Marcy isn't attractive. I like her just fine. It's just that when I'm down on her and I call out her name or think it, I inevitably think of this seven-year-old girl I used to know when I was a kid. Her name was Marcy, too. She had freckles, big round glasses and a lisp. My Marcy doesn't have freckles, glasses, or a lisp. She has long black hair that's dry and bugs me sometimes because it gets everywhere. When I wake up in the morning I always have some of it in my mouth. So it's not like I think they're the same person. It's just her name that reminds me of the other. Marcy is a curse. The name, I mean. I think I even told Marcy this at some point. She wasn't amused.

She looks at me from behind her *People* magazine and

asks me if I think it will last between Jennifer Aniston and Brad Pitt. I shrug my shoulders, lean over to turn up the volume on *Family Feud*.

"Survey says ..."

Marcy hates this show. Who is Jennifer Aniston?

Marcy crumples the magazine up and throws it on the floor. "I can't believe it!"

She gets up off the sofa and walks around the room. "There's an article about this couple and their seven kids who won three-million dollars in a lottery and, in less than two years, they were broke. Can you believe it? Flat out of money." She throws her hands up in the air. "Blew it all! Can you imagine the stupidity of people like that?"

I raise my eyebrow. "People make mistakes, honey. You gotta think about where they come from. Not everyone knows they should invest their money. What would you have done? What was it — two million?"

"Three! I wouldn't buy a fur coat, that's for damn sure."

Marcy goes to the window and looks outside. It's a sunny mid-July day. She presses her left hand to the window pane. I look back to the television set. Whatever happened to Richard Dawson?

"Honey, let's rob a bank."

"Top five answers on the board ..."

"Gary, did you hear me?"

Before I know it, Marcy is on top of me, her face plastered against mine, breathing my air.

"Oh come on, Gary. It would be so easy. All we'd have to do is find a bank in some mall where they know everybody who comes in. We'll be strangers. And we'll be in disguise, so they won't have any way to identify us. By the time anyone got to us we would have changed our clothes."

"Why don't you just buy lottery tickets like every one else? Besides, it's too dangerous. Where would we get a gun?"

"Marshall has a gun. So does Amanda. She got one after the rape attempt. I don't blame her, either. This city isn't safe."

"And you want to rob a bank? I can't believe you, today."

I recognize the look on her face. It's the same one she had when she wanted us to move in together, when she brought home a stray cat, when the porn shop had a sale on dildos, and when she decided to have an abortion. That don't-fuck-with-me look.

"Clowns."

"Huh?"

"We'll dress up like clowns!"

"Didn't they make a movie about that with Bill Murray?"

"Yeah. So?"

"Didn't it die at the box office?"

"So? It did well on video."

"So did *Body of Evidence*. That doesn't mean we should all burn our lovers with candle wax. Come on, clowns?"

"Gary, nobody's going to help us; we've got to help ourselves."

"By robbing a bank? Why not sign up for some kind of career-development program at the office? Ask for a raise?"

"You're no fun at all," she says, getting up and walking away. She turns off the TV. "And we're the only people I know who don't have a remote control."

"So robbing a bank is fun, now?"

"It could be!" She turns back to me with a hopeful grin. "Oh Gary, don't you see that this could make such a difference in our lives?"

"Yeah, right. Like the time you tried to stick a vibrator up my ass because you said our sex was boring?"

"I enjoyed it."

"We could go to prison if we got caught."

"But our life is a prison …"

"Oh great, Marcy. That really motivates me to want to rob a bank."

"We could buy that new Ella Fitzgerald boxed set."

Evil. Marcy is evil.

"And we might even be able to find that Billie Holliday boxed set they put out a few years ago, on CD. I'm sure there's one somewhere in this city. Come on, Gary. I know how much you want it."

She's teasing me now. She knows I'd do anything for that boxed set. Three-hundred dollars. Sixteen CDs. Two-hundred-and-forty songs. Ella … And possibly Billie, too.

She's only just begun to apply the white makeup to my face and I'm already breaking out in a sweat. We're in the back of a rented van without air conditioning (mistake number one), dressed in the rented clown costumes (mistake number two), in oppressive July heat in Mississauga (mistake number three), and about to rob a bank (mistake number four). How we're going to manage to pull this thing off is beyond me.

The last few weeks have been insufferable. Marcy'd taken to playing all three of my Ella Fitzgerald CDs incessantly. She played "Black Coffee" each morning as I drank my java (with cream and sugar) before going to the office. She played "Summertime." When it rained, it was "Stormy Weather." If it was nice out, she'd play "On the Sunny Side of the Street" until I wanted to hurl the stereo out the window.

When we argued about details of the heist, Marcy would rush to put on "Mood Indigo." If we had sex – if – late at night, you can rest assured that "Midnight Sun" was playing quietly in the living room. Over and over until I couldn't concentrate, and, instead of my Marcy, I'd see the seven-year-old Marcy with her oversized white-framed glasses, the ugly, dirty-blonde pageboy and freckles. Sometimes I'd imagine the freckles moving like liquid over the surface of her skin. And if I listened carefuly, I was sure I heard a steady hiss coming from her mouth. Not a sibilant *sss* sound, but a lisp. *Lithen carefully. Whatth that thound?* I'd lose my erection and retreat to the bench outside our building. Then I would hear strains of "Solitude" floating above me.

My nerves are frayed. I've become so irritable that I'll

pounce on anyone whistling "A-Tisket A-Tasket." How I'd love to forget "These Foolish Things" we've been planning and bludgeon Marcy with "Mack The Knife." Why couldn't I have a thing for Tennessee Ernie Ford? He'll never put out a boxed set.

◊   ◊   ◊

Marcy secures the bright-red ball on my nose and then pulls back, smiling a real smile under the greasepaint.

"You look great." She checks herself in a small hand-held mirror and then places it back beside her on the floor. "Now, you haven't forgotten anything, have you?"

"No."

"Tell me the plan."

"Again?"

"Yes. Again. Don't you want those fucking CDs?"

"Oh! So this is all for me, is it?"

She softens. "Oh Gary, honey … I'm sorry. I'm just a bit nervous, that's all. I'm sorry. But go over the plans once more and then we'll get this whole thing over with."

I sigh. "We go to the front of the bank and you pull the batons out of your bag of tricks. You start to juggle. I go into the bank with my own bag as soon as there is no lineup …"

"And that shouldn't be a problem out here in the middle of summer."

"Right. So then I go in and fill out a withdrawal slip and write the hold-up note on it. I go to a teller and smile as I give her the slip."

"What about the gun? The gun?"

"I whisper to the teller that I have a gun. And a whoopie cushion and a flower that squirts water, blah, blah, blah, blah. Then I take the money and put it in the bag and by this point you've pulled the van up front and I jump in and we drive away and head for the nearest record store. And when this whole episode is over I'll probably wind up being so revolted that I'll get hives whenever I hear Ella Fitzgerald."

"Don't be ridiculous," Marcy purrs, rubbing my arm with her gloved hand. "And we'll have some extra money so we can take a vacation this winter."

"Let's just get it over with, okay? I'm sweating to death in this bloody costume."

Marcy turns around and pushes the back door of the van open. She picks up her big purple bag of tricks and jumps out.

"Alright Chuckles, let's do it!"

I follow, ready for action. We walk toward the bank. We chose The New Bank of Commerce, for revenge. They refused to refund me some outrageous service charges several years ago. I'll get even with them now.

We stop in front of the bank. Marcy plops her bag of tricks on the ground and pulls out three blue batons.

"Nervous?" she asks.

"Not any more. I just pissed myself."

"Good thing I made you put on those Depends. You'd be slipping all over the place." She laughs.

"Ha ha."

"Break a fright wig," she wishes as I turn.

"You're just making this worse."

She pushes me with the end of one of the batons and I stumble toward the door, red bag slung over my shoulder. Out of the corner of my eye I see a woman with a young girl approaching Marcy. She greets them and asks if they'd like to see some tricks. I wait until she starts juggling. She's good! I pull the door open, and feel a blast of cold air on my sweaty face as I step inside.

I orient myself. There's the desk with the deposit and withdrawal slips. I move toward it, bobbing my head from side to side and waving at one of the tellers. It's an older woman who has obviously given up on life. She sports a nifty forest-green pantsuit and has glasses dangling from her neck on one of those gold chains. She gives me a vacant stare. I plop my sack down at the desk and pull a withdrawal slip out of the slot.

This isn't so bad. I turn the piece of paper over, grab the pen-on-a-chain with a pink-gloved hand, and move the pen to the slip.

This is no jo

Shit! The pen runs out of ink. Next time, we've got to find a way to rob an instant teller. I turn to my left and catch a glimpse of Marcy and her small audience outside. I reach for the other holder, but the pen's gone. I crumple up the withdrawal slip and move to the next desk.

To my surprise, this one has a pen that works ...

This is no joke.

Give me all of your mon ...

Something distracts me. I'm not sure what it is. I lift my head up and glance to my left and right but don't see anything. I look back down at the slip before me.

    ... **ey.**

    Don't push the alarm or even ...

Then I know what it is. It's the Muzak system playing something horrifying, something catastrophic. I drop the pen and start shaking, singing along in my mind with that lush, throaty voice that has haunted my dreams for years ...

    Right to the end

    Just like a friend

    I tried to warn you somehow ...

It's "Who's Sorry Now?" from *The Intimate Ella* album. Oh my God. Oh my God.

    You had your way

    Now you must pay ...

I turn to face the tellers, feeling a volcanic eruption in my stomach. I see Marcy in my peripheral vision. She's blowing up a red balloon and twisting it into different shapes.

I hear a police siren in the distance. They already know I'm trying to rob the bank and they're on their way. They'll throw me in jail. I'll never get to see my kids again. I'll never be able to confess to my dying father that I stole his *Penthouse* magazines from his workroom all those years ago. I'll never ... Never mind that. I don't have any children. And my father is a priest. He doesn't even have a workroom. But I'm going to rot in jail!"

    I'm glad that you're sorry now.

"Ith there thomething wrong, thir?" a voice taps at my consciousness and pulls me out of my stupor. Somehow, I've moved to the first wicket. As I stand in front of a pimply-faced teller with short sandy blonde hair and huge, round glasses who is lisping at me, I realize that not only this is the original Marcy (although slightly older than I imagined), but that the police siren has come and gone in a matter of seconds. Passed me by.

"Uh."

"Are you thure you're at the right branch, mithter?

"Uh. Yeah. None of your pens work."

She gives me a quizzical look and offers me a pen. A Bic, medium point, black ink. My favourite. I look outside. Marcy is standing alone now, glaring at me. I can feel her anger, but I can't move. I can't do anything but shout ...

"Okay, I've got a gun!"

"A water gun?" the girl says, mocking me.

Just then I see a blue-and-pink bag sitting on a desk behind the service counter. An HMV bag. It holds something that looks like a box.

"What's in that bag?" I scream at her.

She turns around and looks at the bag and then back at me. "Oh it'th the Ella Fitthgerald thongbook collection."

"Boxed set?"

"Yeah, I jutht bought it ..."

I scream. The teller in the forest-green pantsuit looks over at me with mild disgust, as if I'd just belched or passed wind. It's clear that nobody feels threatened or even has the slightest notion that I am trying to rob this bank.

"What's the matter, got something against Ella Fitzgerald?" the pantsuit teller asks in her caved-in voice.

I shake my head. "No! No, I don't ..." I turn and look outside again, but this time Marcy is gone.

"Alright! I'm robbing this bank!" I say, pointing my gloved hand at the young teller. She smiles at me. Of course. There's no gun in my hand. I turn and take several steps back, grabbing my bag o' tricks and wrestling with it to find the gun. I find the gun. I want to shoot the lisping teller just to prove that it isn't a water gun, but I'm not a violent person. At least, I didn't used to be ...

"And don't laugh at me! I'm a desperate man."

"You're a desperate clown," replies the pantsuit teller. "Why not find another line of work? We're hiring."

Marcy the teller pushes her glasses up the bridge of her nose and then focuses on me. She catches me staring at the HMV bag.

"You want it?"

"*What?!*"

"The Ella Fitthgerald thee dee."

"That's why I'm robbing this fucking bank in the first fucking place!" I feel relieved somewhat now that I've finally said it. "Who can afford a three-hundred-dollar fucking CD? How could you afford it? My wife and I both have jobs and we can't afford it!"

"It'th a part-time job," she says. "I live at home. Dithpothable income."

"Oh, Christ! There's a sixteen-year-old part-time bank teller who can afford it and we can't!" I think I've started hyperventalating. Where is Marcy?

"It was on thale."

It was on sale ...

I wipe my arm across my forehead, dislodging my green fright wig and smearing makeup on the sleeve. I've probably ruined the costume. I start to cry, without control or remorse. Loudly. The young teller turns away and reappears in front of the counter a moment later with the HMV bag in her hands. She extends it toward me.

"Here," she says. "Why don't you take thith? You obviouthly need it more than me."

I stand silently for a moment, wondering how ridiculous I look. I reach my left hand up and pull off the curly green wig. "Really?"

"Why not? Go on. Take it. Jutht don't hurt anyone."

Possessed by a force I cannot recognize or understand, I step forward and take the bag. I drop my wig on the floor and place the gun on the counter and edge it toward the bespectacled girl. Stepping back, I look outside. Still no sign of Marcy. But I am somehow liberated. I have revealed myself and discarded my weapon. I've surrendered to the gentler forces of nature. And what need do I have for a partner who manipulates and forces me into violent crime? Marcy is gone. History. Outta here.

"Thank you," I say to the girl. "Thank you very much. I think you've done something wonderful here today." Tears stream from my eyes.

"Hurry up now," she says, "before the polithe come. And enjoy the muthic."

"Thank you," I say. "I will."

I walk out of the bank with the HMV bag in my hand. I start ripping and pulling at my clothing, at the costume which can no longer disguise me. I remove the suit, wipe

my face with it and leave the crumpled rags on the
ground.

Wearing only my Depends, I crouch down, open the
bag, and remove the glorious boxed set. Mega Ella. There
is a piece of paper taped to the top of the box. As I glance
at it, I hear the sound of an engine approaching.

Happy Birthday, Gary,
You're worth all this to me and more.
Love,
Marcy
XOXO

Michael Rowe photo

ROBERT THOMSON's short stories have appeared in several anthologies – including *Queer View Mirror 1* and *2* and *Brothers of the Night* – and in his first book, *Secret Things*. He lives in Toronto.